The Short Stories of Letitia Elizabeth Landon

Volume I

Letitia Elizabeth Landon was born on the 14th August 1802 in Chelsea, London.

A precocious child she had her first poem published is 1820 using the single 'L' as her marker. The following year her first volume appeared and sold well. She published a further two poems that same year with just the initials 'L.E.L." It provided the basis for much intrigue.

She became the chief reviewer of the Gazette and published her second collection, 'The Improvisatrice', in 1824.

By 1826, rumours began to circulate that she had had affairs. For several years they continued to circulate until she broke off an engagement when her betrothed, upon further investigation, found them to be unfounded. Her words reflect the lack of trust she felt "The mere suspicion is dreadful as death"

On June 7th 1838 she married George Maclean, initially in secret, and a month later they sailed to the Cape Coast.

However, the marriage proved to be short lived as on October 15th, that same year, Letitia was found dead, a bottle of prussic acid in her hand.

Index of Contents

ISADORE

In the town church-yard there is a grave covered with a plain slab of white marble, with no other inscription than "Isadore d'Ereillo, aged nineteen." These few words speak histories for the heart; they tell of a beautiful flower withered, far from its accustomed soil, in the spring day of its blossom; they tell the fate of a young and unhappy stranger, dying in a foreign country, remote from every early association, her last moments unsoothed by affectionate solictitude,—no tender voice, whose lightest sound breathed happy memories, no eye of fondness on which the fainting mourner might look for sympathy—her very ashes separated from their native earth.

"Might I not fancy myself a hero of fiction?" said Colonel Fitzallan, bending gracefully as he caught the small snow hand which had just arranged his sling; "Fair lady, henceforth I vow myself your true and loyal knight, and thus pledge my heart's first homage!" pressing the yielding fingers gently to his lips. Alas, thought Isadore, while those eloquent interpreters of the feelings, a blush, sigh, and smile, mingled together—he loves not passionately as I love, or he could not trifle thus; a light compliment was never yet breathed by love. Isadore was at that age when the deeper tenderness for woman first deepens the gaiety of childhood, like the richer tine that dyes the rose as it expands into summer loveliness. Adored by her father, for she had her mother's voice and look and came a sweet remembrance of his youth's sole warm dream of happiness, of that love whose joy departed ere it knew one cloud of care, or one sting of sorrow; a word of anger seemed to Don Fernando a sacrilege against the dead, and his own melancholy constancy gave a reality to the romantic imaginings of his child. She now loved Fitzalla with all the fervour of first excited attachment: she had known him under circumstances the most affecting, when the energies and softer feelings of woman were alike called forth; when the proud and fearless soldier became dependent on her he had protected; laid on the bed of sickness; far from the affectionate hands that would have smoothed, the tender eyes that would have wept o'er his pillow. Isadore became his nurse, soothed with unremitting care the solitude and weariness of a sick-room; and when again able to bear the fresh air of heaven, her arm was the support of her too interesting patient. With Fitzallan the day of romance was over; a man above thirty cannot enter in the wild visions of an enthusiastic girl; flattered by the attachment which Isadore's every look betrayed, he trifled with her, regardless or thoughtless of the young and innocent heart that confided so fearlessly. Love has no power to look forward—the delicious consciousness of the present, a faint but delightful shadow of the past, form its eternity; the possibility of separation never entered the mind of his Spanish love, till Fitzallan's instant return to England became necessary. They parted with all those gentle vows which are such sweet anchors for hope to rest on in absence—but alas such frail ones. For a time her English lover wrote very regularly. That philosopher knew the human heart who said, "I would separate from my mistress for the sake of writing to her." A word, a look, may be forgotten; but a letter is a lasting memorial of affection. The correspondence soon slackened on his part. Isadore, tending the last moments of a beloved parent, had not one thought for self; but when that father's eyes were closed, and her tears had fallen on the grave of the companion of her infancy, the orphan looked round for comfort, for consolation, and felt, for the first time, her loneliness and the sickness of hope deferred. Fear succeeded expectation; fear, not for his fidelity but his safety: was he again laid on the bed of sickness, and Isadore far away?—She dwelt on this idea, till it became a present reality; suspense was agony: at length she resolved on visiting England. She sailed, and, after a quick voyage, reached the land;—a wanderer seeking for happiness, which, like the shadow thrown by the lily on the water, still eludes the grasp. It was not thus in the groves of Arragon she looked forward to the British shore; it was then the promised home of a beloved and happy bride. The day after her arrival in London, she drove to her agent's (for her father, during the troubles in Spain, had secured some property in the English funds,) hoping from him to gather some intelligence of the Colonel. Passing through a very crowded street, her coach becoming entangled in the press, occasioned a short stoppage. Gazing round in that mood, who, anxious to escape the impressions within, the eye involuntarily seeks for others without, her attention became attracted to an elegant equipage. Could she be mistaken?—never in that form—it was surely Fitzallan! Well she remembered that graceful bend, that air of protection with which he supported his companion. The agitated Spaniard just caught a glimpse of her slight and delicate figure, of eyes blue as a spring sky, of a cheek of sunset; and, ere her surprise allowed the power of movement, the carriage was out of sight. Her entreaties to be allowed to alight, being only attributed to fear, were answered by assurances that she was safe. Gradually becoming more composed, she bade the coachman inquire who lived in the house opposite—it was the name she longed to hear—Colonel Fitzallan. She returned home, and with a tremulous hand traced a few lines, telling him how she had wept his silence, and entreating him to come and say she was till his own Isadore. The evening passed drearily away; every step made the colour flush her cheek; but he came not. Was he indispensably engaged? Had he not received her note?—any supposition but intentional delay. The next morning, the same fevered anxiety oppressed her: at length she heard the door, and, springing to the window, caught sight of a military man—she heard his step on the stairs, a gentleman entered, but it was not Fitzallan! Too soon she learnt his mission; he whom she had so loved, so trusted, had wedded another—the lady she saw the day before was his wife; and, unwilling to meet her himself, he had charged a friend to communicate the fatal intelligence. Edward B— gazed with enthusiastic admiration on the beautiful creature, whose pale lip, and scalding tears, which forced their way through the long dark eyelashes, belied the firmness her woman's pride taught her to assume. Shame, deep shame, thought he, on the cold, the mercenary spirit which could thus turn the warm feelings of a fond and trusting girl into poisoned arrows, could thus embitter the first sweet flow of affection. He took her hand in silence—he felt that consolation in a case of this kind was but mockery. They parted, the one to despair over the expired embers, the other to nurse the first sparkles of hope. The next morning, scarcely aware what he was doing, or of the motive which actuated him (for who seeks to analyze love's earliest sensations?) Edward sought the abode of the interesting stranger. He found her with Colonel Fitzallan's solicitor; that gentleman, suspicious of the warm feeling evinced by his friend for the fair Spaniard, had employed a professional man; for he was well aware that the letters he had written would give Isadore strong claims upon him. He arrived at the moment when she first comprehended her lover's reason for wishing his letters restored, originated in his fear of a legal use being made of them. Her dark eyes flashed fire, her cheek burnt with emotion, her heart-beat became audible, as she hastily caught the letters, and threw them into the flames. "You have performed your mission," exclaimed she; "leave the room instantly." Her force was now exhausted, she sank back on the sofa. The tender assiduities of Edward at length restored her to some degree of composure. It was luxury to have her feelings entered into; to share sorrow is to soothe it. She told him of hopes blighted for ever, of wounded affection; of the heart sickness which had paled her cheek, and worn to shadow her once symmetrical form. She had in her hand a few withered leaves. "It is," said she, "the image of my fate; this rose fell from my hair one evening; Fitzallan placed it in his bosom; by moonlight I found it thrown aside, it was faded, but to me it was precious from even that momentary caress; I have to this day cherished it. Are not our destinies told by this flower? His was the bloom, the sweetness of love; my part was the dead and scentless leaves." Edward now became her constant companion; she found in him a kind and affectionate brother. At length he spoke of love. Isadore replied by throwing back her long dark hair with a hand whose dazzling whiteness was all that remained of its former beauty, and bade him look on her pale and faded countenance, and there seek his answer. "Yes, I shall wed, but my bridal wreath will be cypress, my bed the grave, my spouse the hungry worm!" Edward gazed on her face, and read conviction; but still his heart clung to her with all the devotedness of love, which hopes even in despair, and, amid the wreck of every promise of happiness, grasps at even the unstable wave. One evening she leaned by a window, gazing fixedly on the glowing sky of a summer sunset: the rich colour of her cheek, which reflected the carnation of the west, the intense light of her soft but radiant black eyes, excited almost hope: could the hand of death be on what was so beautiful? For the first time she asked for her lute; hitherto, she had shrunk from the sound of music; Fitzallan had loved it; to her it was the knell of departed love. She waked a few wild and melancholy notes. "These sounds," sighed she, "are to me fraught with tender recollections; it is the vesper hymn of my own country." She mingled her voice with the tones, so faint, so sad, but so sweet, it was like the song of a spirit as the concluding murmur died away. She sunk back exhausted; Edward for a while supported her head on his shoulder; at length he parted the thick curls from off her face, and timidly prest her lips;—he started from their chilling touch—it was his first, his last kiss—Isadore had expired in his arms!

THE INDIAN ORPHAN

Surely there are
Some stars whose influence is upon our lives
Evil and overpowering: it is those
That blight the young rose in its earliest spring;
Sully the pearl fresh from its native sea;
Wing the shaft to the youthful warrior's breast
In his first field; and fade the crimson cheek
And blue eyes of the beautiful.
L. E. L.

Yes, I remember well how she would sit of an evening and watch the sky, while her eyes flashed with light, as wild, as intense, as the brightest star on which she gazed; and when my kiss awakened her from her dream, I remember too, the warm heavy tears that were on the cheek she pressed to mine. "Thou art not like thy mother, my fair child," she would exclaim; "may thy life be unlike hers too!" and the words came forth so gently, and her voice was so sweet! I better loved to sit by her knee, and listen to her sad soft song, than to chase the fairest butterfly that lay like a gem on the roses I delighted to water. But my mother's voice grew feeble, and darkness settled on her eyes; her lip was pale and parched, and when I hung on her neck, she told me she was sick and faint, and wept: she would lie for hours on the mat, and an old woman who came to see us sometimes, said she was dying. Dying!—I knew not what she meant, but I felt sad, very sad, and went and lay down by my mother; but the hand I took was burning, and the pressure was so slight I scarcely felt it.

It was a beautiful summer sunset,—not those soft gradual tints which melt on the evenings I have since seen in England; but the sunset of a southern clime, all passion, all flame—the sky was crimson; the Ganges was crimson too; its waves flashed through the green foliage that overshadowed it, like the gush of red meteors through the midnight clouds. My mother called me to her; I knelt by the mat, while she told me to look on the glorious sky, and said it was the last she should ever see; that like that sun she was passing to darkness and silence, but not like that sun to return. She said she looked for the arrival of a stranger; and if he came after her spirit had fled—"My child, you will remember your mother's last words—tell him I have loved him even unto death; my latest prayer was his name and thine." She leant back, and gasped fearfully, then lay quiet as if she slept, yet her eyes were open and fixed upon me. I remember yet, how I trembled before that cold and appalling look. It grew dark; I lay down close to her side and fell asleep. The morning sun was looking cheerfully forth when I awoke:—my mother lay so still, so motionless, that I believed her to be yet sleeping, but her eyes wide open and bent on me, tempted me to kiss her; even at this moment the chill of that touch is upon my lips. For the first time I shrank from her; I spoke, but she answered not; I took her cold hand, but instantly loosed it: it fell from mine—she had said she was dying—could this be death? I felt a wild, vague conviction that we were separated for ever; but the very despair of separation brought with it the hope of reunion; I might die too.

I was repeating, with incoherent rapidity, "My mother, let me die with you!" one arm round the neck of the corpse, the other fanning backwards and forwards, to keep away the flies, and my cheek resting upon hers, when the door of the hut opened, and a stranger entered. I looked up with wonder, not unmixed with pleasure: the splendour of his scarlet and gold dress, the white waving plumes of his helmet, soon attracted a child's attention; but child as I was, one glance at his face fastened my gaze. The deep crimson of exercise had given place to a hue of ghastly whiteness; every feature was convulsed; his deep broken sobs as he sat by the bed, his face covered with his hands, yet startle my memory: at last I remembered my mother's words, and hesitatingly approached him, and repeated them. He started, and clasped me in his arms. I felt his tears on my face; he seemed kind, yet fear was my principal sensation, as wringing my hands and my mother's together, he said in words scarcely audible: "Abra, my care of our child shall atone for my desertion of thee!" Others, his attendants, now came in: to one of these he gave me in charge; but when they strove to raise me from the body, I struggled in their hold, and grasped a hand, and implored my mother to keep me. I was, however, carried away, weeping the first tears of sorrow I had ever shed.

My course of life was completely changed: I was placed in the family of a Mr. and Mrs. L—. They had many children of their own, educated under their own roof; to my father it therefore appeared a most eligible situation: to me it was one of unceasing mortification, of unvaried unhappiness. Mr. and Mrs. L—. considered me as an incumbrance, which their obligations to Mr. St. Leger did not allow them to throw off; and their children as a rival, though from my being the daughter of an Indian, as a being inferior to all. But this very repelling of my best affections caused them to flow the more strongly where their current was not checked; the memory of my mother was to me the heart's religion; my love to my father was the sole charm of existence. I grew up a neglected, solitary, and melancholy girl, affectionate from nature, reserved from necessity; when I was suddenly summoned to attend the death-bed of my father. He breathed his last in my arms. I never left the corpse—I watched the warmth, the last colour of life depart, till the hand became ice, the cheek marble. He was buried in his uniform; my hand threw the military cloak over his face: even when they nailed down the coffin I remained, though every blow struck on my heart as the farewell to happiness, the last words of hope. They bore the corpse away; and as the physician forbade my attendance at the funeral, I watched the procession as it passed the window. The muffled drums, the dead march, seemed sounds from the grave; stately figures paced with slow and solemn steps; with their arms and eyes bent down silently to the earth, I saw them move onward; I lost the sound of the heavy measured tread, I only caught a distant tone of the now faint music. I sprang forward in desperate eagerness; the sun was at noon; my head was uncovered, yet I felt not the heat: I followed, and reached the grave as they were lowering the body to its long, last home. The whole scene swam before me, and I was carried back insensible by some who recognised me. On my recovery I was coldly informed that my father's property, left wholly mine, insured me a small, but independent fortune; and that his will expressed a wish for my immediate departure for England, assigned to the care of a Mrs. Audley, a distant relation of his. Every thing was prepared for my departure: an orphan, with not one either to love or be loved by, I was perfectly indifferent to my future destiny. The evening before I embarked, I went to bid farewell to my father's grave; there was a storm gathering on the sky, and the hot still air and my own full heart, oppressed me almost to suffocation. There was no light, save from the fireflies which covered the mansion, or from the dim reflection of the red flames which had been kindled on the banks of the river. I reached the grave; the newly turned-up earth of its mound was close to another, where the green grass grew in all its rank luxuriance. I looked upon the plain white stone; it was, as my heart foretold, graven with my mother's name, which had hitherto been concealed from me. I sat down; tears of the most soothing gratitude fell over the graves; I felt so thankful that they were united in death. It was to me happiness, that earth had yet something to which I could attach myself; only those who have wept over the precious sod which contains all they loved, all they worshipped, can tell how dear are these lonely dwellings of the departed. I knelt, prayed, wept, and kissed the clay of each parent's grave by turns; and only the red light of the morning warned me to depart. I went home and slept, and the fearful dream of my feverish slumber yet hangs upon me. I was alone, in a dark and wild desert; the ground beneath was parched, yet the sky was black, and red streaks of light passed over it. I heard the hiss of serpents, the howl of savage beasts; my lips were dry and hot; my feet burned as they pressed the fiery sand; and my heart beat even to agony; when suddenly freshness and sweetness breathed around—there came sounds of music and delightful voices; bright and beautiful forms gathered on the air; I found myself in a green and blessed place. Two came towards me—my father, my mother! they embraced me, and I awoke soothed, with their smile visible before me, their blessing yet breathing in my ears. The next day I embarked, and we set sail immediately; yet I had time to contrast my own forlorn neglectedness with the lot of others; and bitterly did I feel the kind farewells, the blessings implored on my companions. I envied them even the sorrow of parting.

At length the sun set in the waters, and till the final close of the evening I lingered by the side of the vessel. It was a calm sky: not a shadow was on the face of heaven, not a breeze ruffled the sleeping waves, no sound nor motion broke the deep repose; but repose was at this moment irksome to my soul. Was I the only one disturbed and agitated? A cloud, a breath of wind, would have been luxury—they would have seemed to enter into my feelings, to take away my sense of utter loneliness. I left the deck, for there were hurried steps around, and my idleness weighed upon me like a reproach; I felt useless, insignificant; there were glad voices talking close by my side—there were tones of hope, exultation, sorrow, and affection—I could sympathise with none of them. I hastily threw open the window of the cabin, and saw the country I was leaving for ever, like a line in the air, and all but lost in the horizon. No one can say farewell with indifference; and there I leant, gazing on the receding land anxiously, nay even fondly, till darkness closed around and I could no longer even fancy I saw it. Lost in that vague, but painful reverie, when the mind, too agitated to dwell on any one subject, crowds past sorrows and future fears upon the overburthened present, time had passed unheeded, and the moon, now risen, made the coast visible again. It must be agony to the heart to say a long, and it may prove an eternal farewell, to all connected with us by every link of early association and affection of many years' standing; to the mother whose smile was the light of our childhood; to the father whose heart goes with us; to all who have shared in our joys and our griefs; this, indeed, must be an overflowing of the cup of affliction; but even this painful accumulation of feeling was preferable to mine of single and complete isolation. It is soothing to reflect, that we are dear to those we leave behind; that there are some who will treasure our memory in the long hours of absence, and look forward to our meeting again; for never does the moment of reunion rise so forcibly on the mind as at that of separation. These thoughts are like rain drops in the season of drought, but I looked on the land of my birth, and knew there was not one to call a blessing on her far away; not one to wish the wanderer's return; the cold earth lay heavily on the hearts that would have throbbed at my departing; the eyes that would have wept were sealed by death, in the home of darkness and forgetfulness, where joy and sorrow are alike.

The voyage appeared short, for I had no thing to anticipate, and the glories of the ocean suited my feelings, I have looked on the face of nature with love and with wonder; but never have I had that intense communion with her beauties which I have had at sea. At last the white cliffs of England came in sight: they were hailed with a shout of delight; it had no echo in my heart. But it was when we arrived in port that I more than ever felt how very lonely I was; the whole ship was bustle, confusion, and happiness; numbers were every moment crowding the deck—there was the affectionate welcome, the cordial embrace, words of tenderness, still tenderer tears; all was agitation, anxiety, and delight. There was one group in particular, a sailor whose little boy was so grown that he did not at first recognize him—the delight of the child, two inches taller with pleasure—the half affection, half pride, glowing in the fresh island completion of the mother—every kindly pulse of the heart sympathised with them. I felt doubly an orphan as they left the deck. At this moment a young man addressed me, and announcing himself as the son of Mrs. Audley, the lady with whom I was henceforth to live, led me to the boat which waited at the side of the vessel; and a short journey brought us to Clifton and the cottage where Mrs. Audley resided. How vividly the thoughts and feelings which crowded that night about my pillow rise upon my memory! I think it is not saying too much of that natural instinct which attracts us to one person and repels us from another, when I call it infallible. There is truth and certainty in our first impressions; we are so much the creatures of habit, so much governed in our opinions by the opinions of others, we so rarely begin to think till our thoughts are already biased, that our intuitive perception of good and evil, and consequently of friend and foe is utterly neglected. If, in forming our attachments, instead of repeating what we have heard, we recalled our feelings when we first met, there would be fewer complaints than are now of disappointed expectations. First impressions are natural monitors, and nature is a true guide. My impressions were delightful—I slept contented and confiding; and my spirits next day were worthy of the lovely morning that aroused them.

Mrs. Audley's cottage, the landscape, and the sky, were altogether English: the white walls, the green blinds, the open sash-windows, the upper ones hung round with the thick jessamine that had grown up to the roof, the lower ones into which the rose-trees looked; the blinds half-way down, just showing the cluster of red roses and nothing more, though they completely admitted the air, loaded with the breath of the mignonette; while the eyes felt relieved by the green and beautiful, but dim light which they threw over the room. It was like enchantment to step from the cool and shadowy parlour into the garden with its thousand colours, the beds covered with annuals, those rainbows of the spring, the Guelder rose, the laburnums, mines of silver and gold; the fine green turf; but nothing struck me so much as, beneath the shade of an old beech tree, a bank entirely covered with violets. It may seem fanciful, but to me the violet is the very emblem of woman's love; it springs up in secret; it hides its perfume even when gathered; how timidly its deep blue leaves bend on their slight stem! The resemblance may be carried yet further—woman's love is but beautiful in its purity; let the hot breath of passion once sully it, and its beauty is departed—thus as the summer advances, the violet loses its fragrance; June comes, but its odours are fled—the heart too has its June; the flower may remain, but its fragrance is gone for ever. Flowers are the interpreters of love in India, painting in the most vivid but in the softest colours speaking in the sweetest sighs: while each blossom that fades is a mournful remembrancer either of blighted hopes or departed pleasures. I would give my lover violets; the rose has too much display. J'admire les roses, mais je m'attendris sur les violettes. The rose is beauty—the violet tenderness. And the country round was so placidly delightful. I had been used to the sweeping shadow of gigantic trees, to oceans of verdure, to the wide and magnificent Ganges; but the landscape here came with a quiet and feeling of contentment on the heart. I remember so well the first time I ever walked on the Downs! The day had been very showery and the sky was just beginning to clear; the dark gloomy volumes in which the tempest was rolling away were but little removed from clouds of transparent whiteness, and between, like intervals of still enjoyment amid the hopes and fears of life, gleamed forth the deep calm blue of the horizon. Faintly coloured like a dream of bliss, a half-formed rainbow hung on the departing storm, as fearful of yet giving promise of peace. Everything around was in that state of tremulous repose, which succeeds a short and violent rain. The long shadows and double brilliancy of the light from the reflecting raindrops, contrasted in the scenery, like sorrow and joy succeeding tears. Never could the banks of the Avon have been seen to a greater advantage. On one side of the river rose rocks totally bare, but of every colour and every form; on the other side, banks equally high were covered with trees in their thickest foliage; the one Nature's stupendous fortress, the other her magnificent pavilion of leaves. One or two uncovered masses appeared like the lingering footprints of desolation; but in general where the statelier trees had not taken root, the soil was luxuriantly covered with heath, and the golden-blossomed furze. On the left, dew and sunshine seemed wholly to have fallen in vain: riven in every direction, the rocks had assumed a thousand different shapes, in which the eye might trace, or fancy it traced, every variety of ruin, spire, or turret—the mouldering battlement, the falling tower. Here and there a solitary bramble had taken root, almost as bare and desolate as the spot where it grew. The contrast between the banks was like prosperity and adversity. I do think, if ever any body was happy I was, for the next two years. It is strange, though true, that the happiest part of our life, is the shortest in detail. We dwell on the tempest that wrecked, the flood that overwhelmed—but we pass over in silence the numerous days we have spent in summer and sunshine.

Mrs. Audley was to me as a mother, and Edward and I loved each other with all the deep luxury of love in youth. It was luxury, for it was unconscious. Love is not happiness: hopes, pleasure, delicious and passionate moments of rapture—all these belong in love, but not to happiness. Its season of enjoyment is when its existence is unknown, when fear has not agitated, hope has not expanded the flower it but opens to fade, and jealousy and disappointment are alike unfeared, unfelt. The heart is animated by a secret music. Like the Arabian prince, who lived amid melody, perfume, beauty, and flowers, till he rashly penetrated the forbidden chamber; so, when the first sensations of love are analysed, and his mystery displayed, his least troubled, his most alluring dream, is past for ever. Edward was strikingly handsome; the head finely shaped as that of a Grecian statue, with its profusion of thick curls; the complexion beautiful as a girl's, but which the darkly arched eyebrows, the manly open countenance, redeemed from the charge of effeminacy, his eyes (the expression of "filled with light" was not a mere exaggeration when applied to them); and then the perfect unconsciousness, or, I should rather say, the utter neglect of his own beauty. He was destined for a soldier and for India; and perhaps there is no career in life whose commencement affords such scope for enthusiasm. However false the fancies may be of cutting your way to fame and fortune, of laurels, honours, &c. still there is natural chivalry enough in the heart, to make the young soldier indulge largely in their romance. At length the time of his departure came: Edward was too proud to weep when he bade adieu to his mother and me, his affianced bride; but the black curls on his fair forehead were wet with suppressed agitation, and when be threw himself on horseback, at the garden gate, he galloped the animal at his utmost speed; but when he came to a little shadowy lane, apparently shut out from all, I saw from my window that his pace was slackened, and his head bowed down upon the neck of his steed. They say women are more constant than men: it is the constancy of circumstance; the enterprise, the exertion required of men continually force them out of themselves, and that which was at first necessity soon becomes habit— whereas the constant round of employments in which a woman is engaged, require no fatigue of mind or body; the needle is, generally speaking, both her occupation and amusement, and this kind of work leaves the ideas full play; hence the imagination is left at liberty to dwell upon one subject, and hence habit, which is an advantage on the one side, becomes to her an additional rivet.

For months after Edward's departure I was utterly miserable, listless, apathetic—nothing amused me: but I was at length roused from this state of sentimental indolence by a letter from him: he wrote in the highest spirits; his success had been beyond his utmost expectations; and soon, he said, be might hope and look forward to our joining him in India. I have a great dislike to letter-writing: the phrase "she is an excellent correspondent" is to me synonymous with "she is an excellent gossip." I have seen epistles crossed and recrossed, in which I knew not which most to pity—the industry or idleness of the writer. But every one has an exception to his own rule, and so must I; and from this censure, I except letters from those near and dear to us, and far away. A letter then, breathing of home and affection, is a treasure; it is like a memento from the dead, for absence is as death in all but that its resurrection is in this life. I felt a new spirit in existence; I lived for him, I hoped to rejoin him. I delighted to hear my own voice in the songs he was soon to hear; I read with double pleasure, that I might remember what he would like: but above all else, painting became my favourite pursuit; every beautiful landscape, every delicate flower, every striking countenance which I drew, would, I thought, be so many proofs how I had remembered him in absence. I almost regretted the fine cool airs of a summer evening, the low sweet songs of the birds: I could make for him no memorials of them. Another letter came; and soon after we prepared for our embarkation, and a second time I crossed the ocean. The voyage which had seemed so short before, I now thought never-ending; every day the bright shining sea and the blue sky seemed more monotonous; a thousand times did I compare our fate to that of the enchanted damsel, in one of Madame de Genlis' tales, who has been condemned by a most malignant fairy to walk straight forward over an unvarying tract of smooth green turf, bounded only by the clear azure of the heavens. But we reached India at last.

What is there that has not been said of the pleasure of meeting, yet who has ever said all that is felt— the flow of words and spirits, the occasional breaks of deep and passionate silence, the restlessness of utter happiness, the interest of the most trivial detail—and when on our pillow, the hurry of ideas, the delicious, though agitated throbbing of the heart. To sleep is impossible, but how delightful to lie awake! But my first look at Edward, the next morning, made my pillow sleepless again, and sleepless from anxiety. The climate too surely had been slow poison to him; his bright and beautiful colour was gone; the wan veins of his finely turned and transparent temples, had lost the clearness and the hue of health; and often his voice sank to an almost inaudible tone, as if speaking were too great an exertion. Still he himself laughed at our fears, and pressed the conclusion of our marriage. I wished it too, for I felt it was some thing to be his, even in the grave. It was the evening before the day fixed for uniting us, when he proposed to visit a spot I had often sought alone—the grave of my parents. Once or twice during the walk I was startled by his excessive paleness, but again his smile and cheerfulness reassured me. We sat down together silently. I was too sad for words: a little branch of scented flowers in my hand, was quite washed by my tears. A cloud was flitting over the moon, and for a short space it was entirely dark; suddenly the soft clear light came forth more lovely than before. I bade Edward mark how beautifully it seemed to sweep away the black cloud; he answered me not, but remained with his face bowed on his hands. I put mine into them—they were cold: I saw his countenance—it was convulsed in death.

THE MINIATURE

"'No, leave it open to-night, Charles.'

"'But the damp air, dear mother!'

"'Only revives me!'

"The youth left the lattice, and, for a moment, buried his face in his hands behind the curtains of the bed. 'Charles, dear,' said his mother, and again he resumed his station at her side. It was a small low room, whose whitewashed walls and small grate—there was a fire there, though it was July—spoke the extreme of poverty; yet were there some slight marks of that refined taste which lingers after all that once cherished it is gone. On the little table, near the bed, stood a glass filled with flowers; and a box of mignionette in the window touched every breath of air that entered with sweetness. The dim light threw a shadow over the meanness of the place, and softness and quietness hallowed the agony of the hour; for Charles Seymour was looking for the last time on the face of the mother be had idolized—his young, his beautiful mother, whose small exquisite features, and dark length of hair, might rather have suited a lovely sister dying beneath her first sorrow, than one to whom many a year of grief and care would have made the grave seem a hope and a home, but for those she left behind. By her side, in the deep sleep of infancy, healthy, and coloured like the rose, was a child of four years old. 'God help thee, my poor Lolotte!' and the anxiety of a mother's love overcame the quiet of that calm which almost ever precedes the last struggle. 'Alas, Charles! a sorrowful and anxious heritage is yours!'

"'A sacred one, mother !' and, in his heart, he vowed to be father and mother to the orphan child; and thrice tenderly did the cold hand he held press his, as he kissed the little creature so blessed in its unconsciousness.

"Deeper and deeper fell the shadows, and deeper and deeper the silence, when the few clouds that had gathered, gradually broke away, and the room was filled with the clear moonlight. Suddenly there came the sound of martial music—the tramp of measured steps. Mrs Seymour started unaided from her pillow. 'It is the march of your father's regiment—they played it that last morning—for pity's sake, don't let them play it now!' " Her head fell on Charles's shoulder; a strange sound was heard, such as comes from human mouth but once—it was the death-rattle, and a corpse lay heavily on his bosom.

"'Mistress has wanted nothing, I hope?' said an old woman, opening the door gently; one look told her that her mistress would never know earthly want again.

"Disuniter of all affection—awful seal to life's nothingness—warning and witness of power and judgment—Death has always enow of terror and sorrow, even when there are many to comfort the mourner, when the path has been smoothed for the sufferer, and life offers all its best and brightest to soothe the survivor; even then, its tears are the bitterest the eye can ever shed, and its misery the deepest heart can ever know. But what must it be when poverty has denied solace even to the few wants of sickness; and when the grave, in closing, closes on the only being there was to love us in the cold wide world?

"Charles Seymour stood by while the old woman laid out the body, and paused in her grief to admire so beautiful a corpse. He had to let his little sinter sleep in his arms, for their mother was laid out on their only bed; he had to order the coffin in which himself placed the body; their short and scant meals were taken in presence of the dead; he heard them drive the nails in the coffin, be stood alone by the grave, and wept his first tears when he reflected that he had not wherewithal to pay for even a stone to mark the spot.

"He went home to meet a talkative broker, who came to buy their two or three articles of furniture; and he leant by the window, in a room empty of everything, but a little bed for his sister, who had crept to his side, with that expression of fear and wonder so painful to witness on the face of a child; and Charles Seymour was but just sixteen. " His father had fallen in the battle of the Pyrenees, and his mother was left with the bare pension of a captain's widow, only one week before the banker, where all their private fortune was deposited, had failed. A few months brought Mrs Seymour to the brink of destitution and the grave; her pension died with her, and Charles was left, with the poor Lolotte, entirely dependent on the small salary be received as clerk in Mr Russel's office; and even this poor situation had been procured for him by the chance interest he had inspired in the apothecary, who had, from mere humanity, attended his mother. His future prospects destroyed—confined to his desk the whole day—debarred from intellectual acquirement—shut out from his former pursuits—with all the feelings of birth and station strong within him, young Seymour would have despaired, but for his sister; for her sake he exerted himself; for her sake he hoped. They lived on in their little back room over the grocer's shop, kept by the widow of a soldier in his father's regiment; he knew he could confide in the old woman's kindness to the child during his unavoidable absence; and, though it was a long walk night and morning to the city, he thought only how healthy the air of Hampstead was for Lolotte; however weary, he was still the companion of her evening walk, or else was up early to accompany her on the heath. In her he concentred all the pride of better days; she was always dressed with scrupulous neatness; his leisure hours were devoted to giving her something of education, and every indulgence did he deny himself in order to bring her home the pretty toy or book, to reconcile her to the solitude of their lonely chamber; and patiently did the little creature make her own pleasure or employment till his return, and then quite forgot that she had sometimes looked from the window, and thought how merrily the children played in the street.

"Three years had thus passed away, and brought with them but added anxiety. Charles felt that over-exertion was undermining his health; and Lolotte—the graceful, the fairy-like—how little would he be able to give her those accomplishments, for which her delicate hand, her light step, and her sweet voice, seemed made! and worse, how little would they suit her future prospects, if be could! It was her seventh birthday, and he was bringing her a young rose-tree as a present, but he felt languid and desponding— even the slight tree seemed a weight almost too heavy to bear. As he went upstairs, he heard Lolotte talking so gaily—a listener is such a pleasure to a child! He entered, and saw her seated on the knee of an elderly man, in whose face something of sadness was mixed with the joyful and affectionate attention with which he was bending to his pretty companion.

"How a few words change the destiny of a life! A few, a very few words told Charles Seymour that Mr de Lisle, his mother's brother, stood before him, just arrived from India—a few words gave him an almost father, a fortune, and friends; for Mr de Lisle had sought the orphans, to be the children of his heart and his home.

"Another year had passed away. Charles Seymour's brow was still darkened with thought, but not anxiety; and his cheek, though pale, had no hue of sickness. He was seated in the little study, peculiarly his own; books, drawings, papers, were scattered round, and not a favourite author but found a place on his shelves. To-day his solitude was often broken in upon—it was Lolotte's birthday; and a sunny face and buoyant step entered his room, to show the many treasures heaped on that anniversary.

"There was a little female art in this. Lolotte, amid all her gay presents, felt half sorry, half surprised, to find none from her brother. Had he forgotten!—to show him her gifts, might remind him of his own: still, Charles offered her no remembrance of the day. A child's ball was too new and too gay, not to banish all thought but of itself; but when Lolotte went into her room for the night, and saw her table covered with presents, and still none from her brother, it was too much; and she sat down on her little stool, where, when Charles entered, he found her crying.

"'My own sweet sister, you were not forgotten, but my birthday remembrance was too sad a one. I could not spoil your day of pleasure by a gift so sorrowful.'

"He presented her with a little packet, and the cheek which he kissed as he said, Good night, was wet with his tears.

"Lolotte opened the paper—it contained a miniature, and she knew that the beautiful face was that of her mother. It was not till the morning that she saw the following lines were with it:

"Your birthday, my sweet sister,—

What shall my offering be?
Here's the red grape from the vineyard,
  And roses from the tree.

"But these are both too passing,
  Fruit and flowers soon decay,
And the gift must be more lasting
  I offer thee to-day.

"'Tis a joyful day, thy birthday—
  A sunny morn in spring;
Yet thy sweet eyes will be sadden'd
  By the mournful gift I bring.

"Alas! my orphan sister,
  You'll not recall the face,
Whose meek and lovely likeness
  These treasured lines retrace.

"It is your mother's picture;
  You are so like her now—
With eyes of tearful dimness,
  And grave and earnest brow!

"Oh! be like her, my sister!
  But less in face than mind;
I would you could remember
  One so tender and so kind.

"Oh, weep that angel mother!
  Such tears are not in vain;
Yet dry them in the hope, love,
  We all shall meet again.

"And keep this gentle monitor,
  And when you kneel in prayer,
Deem an angel's eye is on you—
  That your mother watches there.

"I'll believe that she rejoices
  O'er her darling child to-day;
God bless thee, dearest sister!
  'Tis all that I can say."

THE BETROTHED

The empress and her daughter stood together: alike, singularly alike, as they were, in height, in the same high, finely-cut features, the same clear blue eyes, the same fair Saxon complexion, yet the likeness, which seemed so strong at the first look, became almost a contrast as that look was prolonged into observation. It was not the difference of age, for the mother's eye was as bright, and her cheek as rich in colour, as her daughter's; but the sweetness which was in Maria Theresa's smile only, was in every line of the archduchess's face. The azure depths of the eyes, in the one, mirrored every thought and every feeling; those of the other expressed but what they chose should appear. Each had the same fair broad forehead; but in the elder one a slight contraction of the brow had become habitual. Both stepped with the stately bearing of a noble race; but Maria Theresa moved as if over the neck of a prostrate world, while Josepha seemed as if she would have turned aside rather than crush the meanest worm on her path. Both were splendidly dressed—the young princess as a bride; the diamond tiara was surmounted by a chaplet of orange flowers, the white velvet train embroidered with pearls, and a veil of silver tissue fell almost to her feet. The bright and gay appearance of the youthful archduchess was little in unison with the rest of the scene. The huge and dark chamber was hung with crimson damask worked with gold; but the gold had been long tarnished, and the brilliancy had passed away from the crimson. Portraits in massive frames, the gilding as dim as the colours, covered the walls. Most of them were garbed in black velvet, according to the Spanish taste, and the heavy brow and thick lip all bespoke their Austrian descent. At the upper end of the room was a purple canopy which had been raised over a temporary altar; towards this the empress led her daughter, and the shadow of the canopy fell dark upon the young bride. A small group gathered round—staid, grave-looking men—who, whatever of fierce passion might be in the heart, had long banished all betrayal of it from the face. The face of the emperor, who, till summoned to give his daughter's hand, stood in the background, was the only one that had aught of the expression of humanity—and that expression was only of its weakness. But where was the bridegroom? Miles and miles away. The royal lover woos by an envoy and wins by a treaty. In his place, his ambassador stood forth—an aged noble man, who, having spent a whole life in the observance of forms, held them to be the highest attributes of human nature.

The ceremony proceeded, and, at its close, the ambassador dropped on his knee and kissed the hand of the Duchess of Parma. Josepha turned, and would have knelt to her mother, but this the empress prevented, and, folding her in her arms, pressed her lips to her brow, and wished her many years of happiness. Very ungracefully, but very affectionately, the emperor pressed forward; by this time he had forgotten all the advantages of the alliance, and every thing but that he was about to lose his favourite child. Maria Theresa evidently endured this display very impatiently; her husband met her eye, and—with that species of experience which must be peculiarly adapted to fools, for it is they who are said to learn by it—read its meaning, and shrunk back into silence and himself. The Marquis di Placentia now gave a signal to an attendant, and a page stepped forward with a casket; its contents the ambassador again knelt to offer to his new sovereign. It was the portrait of the Duke of Parma, fastened to a chain of brilliants. The empress herself took the picture, and placed it round her daughter's neck.

A collation was spread in the adjoining room, and thither the party adjourned. Many others of the court were now admitted to offer their congratulations, and it was late in the day before the Duchess of Parma could be permitted to retire. Weary with fatigue, and oppressed by heat, Josepha gladly withdrew to her own chamber. Summoning her attendants, she hastened to put off her cumbrous dress.

"I will put on my canoness robe," said the duchess; a costume frequently worn both by herself and sisters.

"Nay," exclaimed Pauline, a favourite attendant, "not black upon your wedding-day, it is so very unlucky!"

The princess persisted, and, after helping her on with the loose black silk robe, at her command Pauline withdrew. Josepha seated herself by the open casement, and for the first time gazed on the miniature she wore. The duke's face was one of uncommon beauty and intelligence; the softness of the enamel and the skill of the painter might have added something to the beauty, but you felt the expression was copied, not given. The bride felt a sense of happiness and security steal over her as she watched the open and kindly meaning of the eyes, that seemed to answer to her own. Perhaps, too, the outward influences of the lovely evening-time might give something of their own soothing sweetness. The air came through the window, with the odours of the garden below and the freshness of the dews above— for the heat was melting in a gentle rain. Suddenly a strain of music floated upon the air; it was from a band belonging to the palace, and they played a slow and beautiful Italian air. There were words belonging to the song—Josepha knew them—they spoke of passionate and happy love; she blushed as she glanced at the portrait, and then leaned back, half to listen to the distant tones, and half to dream of the future, as the young dream when hope prophesies by the imagination. She was yet lost in fantasies so vivid that truth itself seemed not so actual, when the door of her apartment slowly opened, and she started from her seat in wonder to see the empress. Maria Theresa was cold and haughty in her general manner; one too who brooked not that her will should meet with question, much less opposition: little marvel was it, therefore, that her child rose with an attitude rather of deference than of affection. But her mother's manner was kind even to softness, and when Josepha drew forwards the large arm-chair she refused it, and, gently taking her daughter's hand, placed herself too in the window-seat.

"Those books are Italian, and the music I hear in the distance is Italian. Ah, my child, even now you are striving to forget us! Alas! our station too much separates those gentler ties which, in lowlier life, bind so closely! How often must I, even to you, my own beloved girl, have seemed stern and severe; for I know a life of anxiety and struggle leaves its own harshness behind. But when, Josepha, in another country you think of your mother, remember with what difficulties that mother has had to contend."

Josepha's only answer was to catch the hand, now placed caressingly amid her beautiful hair, and to cover it with kisses, ay, and also tears.

"A parting like ours," resumed the empress, "is like one beside the grave; let it be in all love and charity. Forgive me, my child, if aught of reproach you have against your mother."

The duchess flung herself at Maria Theresa's feet. "Nay, forgive me, my beloved and revered parent, if ever the petulance of my age has caused me to forget the love and duty I owed! Bless me, my mother!"

"God bless you, my beloved Josepha!" said the empress tenderly and solemnly.

The pause of feeling in both was broken by Maria Theresa looking at the miniature of the Duke of Parma.

"I like the expression of this face—it agrees with what I have heard of his character; and yet, when I think of the distance which will be between, I seem to dread thus trusting your happiness beyond my control. As yet, you know so little the dangers and the difficulties of a position like yours."

"But, my mother," said the duchess, "surely I might be aided by your knowledge."

"The young submit not willingly to be guided by the old, Youth has but a half experience—it has seen but the bright side, and makes no allowance for the coming shadows. How often have I known the sage counsels which would have averted danger treated not only with indifference but even scorn!"

"But not by me," exclaimed her hearer earnestly; "your words will be treasured in my heart like gold."

"My dearest Josepha, I doubt your will to obey as little as I do your love; but I fear the natural thoughtlessness of youth. I could almost now regret that an unwillingness to weigh down the bright brief period of your life has prevented my depressing your young spirits by ever communicating the weight on my own mind. I have been over prudent. I fear you are ill fitted to meet all the exigencies of your novel situation. Beautiful, and with a mind like yours (I have observed its powers, Josepha, more than you may deem), your influence over your husband must be—will be—absolute. Think not, dearest child, that I undervalue your desire to know and follow the right; but oh, that I could give you some of my experience!"

"Can you not, dear mother and sovereign? You know not how reverentially I should hear, and how carefully I should follow, your advice"

This was the very point to which the empress wished to bring her daughter. First kissing the beautiful face which was bent towards her in the earnestness of entreaty, she began speaking. Her natural gifts of persuasion were great; her voice mingled sweetness and firmness; and her smile—it was that for whose sake the gallant chivalry of Hungary swore to die. At first her listener seemed to yield the most earnest and confiding attention; gradually the eloquent countenance of the duchess changed to surprise, wonder, doubt, and finally to almost indignation.

"Say no more!" exclaimed Josepha, throwing herself at the empress's feet: "register every act, penetrate into every thought, of my husband's, to give prompt intelligence of them to the court of Austria!—seek affection the better to betray it! Is this—can this—be my duty to my husband, or my love—"

"Nay," interrupted her mother, repressing the indignation already darkening in her eyes, "I was not prepared for this burst of romance."

"Madam," said the duchess, slowly rising from her knee, "the task of a spy is no task for your daughter."

Her figure was drawn to its utmost height; her brow was contracted; the likeness between herself and her mother was stronger than ever, and in that likeness Maria Theresa saw an end to her well-laid scheme of making the bride of the Duke of Parma a tool in her hands.

"Truly," said she with a scornful smile, "this ducal coronet has turned your head. Wilful and disobedient! We speak on this subject no more."

"Not in anger, my mother," exclaimed Josepha, striving to detain her, "not in anger must you part from me!"

Coldly the empress disengaged her hand: their eyes met—and the young princess staggered back, at the stern and deadly resentment in the pale face of Maria Theresa, and sank on the window-seat.

"It is broken!" said Josepha faintly, as the chain to which hung the portrait of the Duke of Parma fell in glittering fragments at her side. It had caught to the empress's dress, and was shattered. The young duchess leaned against the casement and wept.

To the young it is a very bitter pang to know that their best feelings have been excited merely to be worked upon; but sorrow and shame were soon merged in a vague and terrible fear. The evening came on, and deepened into night. Still, amid the shadows, did Josepha fancy she could see the threatening brow of the empress, pale with anger. Solitude became insupportable, and she called her attendants. But human faces, and human voices, the cheerfulness of the lights, or even her favourite Pauline's bird-like song, were of no avail against the terror which every moment seemed to weigh more heavily on her spirits. With hurried and yet timid steps, starting, though she knew not why, at the least noise, Josepha began to pace the room. A low rap at the door interrupted her walk, and the confessor of the empress entered the apartment. Martini's features were chiselled with the perfection of sculpture, and his high brow bore the impress of mental power and thought far beyond his years, which were yet in their summer; his step was soft and humble—his voice low and sweet; yet fear was the sensation he always inspired. No one ever met his cold and cruel eye—so calm, so colourless—without saying, "That man delights in human misery."

He approached the duchess, and said, as he looked at her black dress, "I rejoice to see, my daughter, you have not waited for me to remind you of the pious duty to-night calls upon you to fulfil."

"What do you mean, father?" said the princess faintly, "I changed my dress on account of the heat."

"I had hoped, my daughter, it was in voluntary humiliation; ill do the gay robes of the bride suit with the meek prayers to be offered in the presence of the dead."

"I pray you to speak your meaning at once!" and Josepha grew pale as marble.

"Your royal highness knows it is your turn to watch and pray by the tomb of the Archduchess Caroline."

Josepha sank fainting against the wainscot of the room.

"The empress will never permit it," cried Pauline, as she sprung to support her mistress; "why, we all know that the archduchess died of the small-pox, and not a creature will enter the chapel."

"I have her grace's commands, who wills that so pious a duty be not neglected. I am sent by her even now to conduct the Duchess of Parma to pay the last duty to her illustrious house."

"Your father—appeal to him," whispered the girl, "but I know that will be of no avail. I conjure you, see your mother yourself!"

"I have seen her," said the duchess, "we parted just now."

Pauline hid her face in her hands.

"I wait your highness's pleasure to conduct you to the chapel."

Josepha rose and prepared to follow.

"I will go with you. At night and alone—it is too terrible!" said the affectionate girl.

"Her highness's vigil must be solitary; thus it has ever been!" replied the priest.

Josepha descended to the chapel; her attendants accompanied her to the door—as it opened it showed the thick hot atmosphere, through which the dim tapers seemed scarcely able to penetrate. The duchess turned round and embraced Pauline, and entered the chapel. They saw her kneel before the altar, and the doors were closed. Late in the night was it before the royal council broke up; then, not till then, did Pauline succeed in conveying the intelligence to the emperor that his favourite daughter had passed the night beside the infectious tomb of her cousin. He rushed himself to the chapel; and there was the duchess as they had left her—kneeling before the altar, and her face bowed in prayer. She had fallen a little forward, so that the steps supported her. They spoke—but she answered not; they raised her in their arms—but found she was dead.

ONE PEEP WAS ENOUGH

All places have their peculiarities: now that of Dalton was discourse—that species of discourse, which Johnson's Dictionary entitles "conversation on whatever does not concern ourselves." Everybody knew what everybody did, and a little more. Eatings, drinkings, wakings, sleepings, walkings, talkings, sayings, doings—all were for the good of the public; there was not such a thing as a secret in the town.

There was a story of Mrs. Mary Smith, an ancient dame who lived on an annuity, and boasted the gentility of a back and front parlour, that she once asked a few friends to dinner. The usual heavy antecedent half-hour really passed quite pleasantly; for Mrs. Mary's windows overlooked the market-place, and not a scrag of mutton could leave it unobserved; so that the extravagance or the meanness of the various buyers furnished a copious theme for dialogue. Still, in spite of Mr. A.'s pair of fowls, and Mrs. B.'s round of beef, the time seemed long, and the guests found hunger growing more potent than curiosity. They waited and waited; at length the fatal discovery took place—that in the hurry of observing her neighbours' dinners, Mrs. Smith had forgotten to order her own.

It was in the month of March that an event happened which put the whole town in a commotion—the arrival of a stranger, who took up his abode at the White Hart: not that there was anything remarkable about the stranger; he was a plain, middle-aged, respectable-looking man, and the nicest scrutiny (and heaven knows how narrowly he was watched) failed to discover anything odd about him. It was ascertained that he rose at eight, breakfasted at nine, ate two eggs and a piece of broiled bacon, sat in his room at the window, read a little, wrote a little, and looked out upon the road a good deal; he then strolled out, returned home, dined at five, smoked two cigars, read the Morning Herald (for the post came in of an evening), and went to bed at ten. Nothing could be more regular or unexceptionable than his habits; still it was most extraordinary what could have brought him to Dalton. There were no chalybeate-springs, warranted to cure every disease under the sun; no ruins in the neighbourhood, left expressly for antiquarians and picnic parties; no fine prospects, which, like music, people make it matter of conscience to admire; no celebrated person had ever been born or buried in its environs; there were no races, no assizes—in short, there was "no nothing." It was not even summer; so country air and fine weather were not the inducements. The stranger's name was Mr. Williams, but that was the extent of their knowledge; and shy and silent, there seemed no probability of learning anything more from himself. Conjecture, like Shakspeare, "exhausted worlds, and then imagined new." Some supposed he was hiding from his creditors, others that he had committed forgery; one suggested that he had escaped from a mad-house, a second that he had killed someone in a duel; but all agreed that he came there for no good.

It was the twenty-third of March, when a triad of gossips were assembled at their temple, the post-office. The affairs of Dalton and the nation were settled together; newspapers were slipped from their covers, and not an epistle but yielded a portion of its contents. But on this night all attention was concentrated upon one, directed to "John Williams, Esq., at the White Hart, Dalton." Eagerly was it compressed in the long fingers of Mrs. Mary Smith of dinnerless memory; the fat landlady of the White Hart was on tip-toe to peep, while the post-mistress, whose curiosity took a semblance of official dignity, raised a warning hand against any overt act of violence. The paper was closely folded, and closely written in a cramped and illegible hand; suddenly Mrs. Mary Smith's look grew more intent—she had succeeded in deciphering a sentence; the letter dropped from her hand. "Oh, the monster!" shrieked the horrified peeper. Landlady and post mistress both snatched at the terrible scroll, and they equally succeeded in reading the following words:—"We will settle the matter to-morrow at dinner, but I am sorry you persist in poisoning your wife, the horror is too great." Not a syllable more could they make out; but what they had read was enough. "He told me," gasped the landlady, "that he expected a lady and gentleman to dinner—oh the villain! to think of poisoning any lady at the White Hart; and his wife, too—I should like to see my husband poisoning me!" Our hostess became quite personal in her indignation.

"I always thought there was something suspicious about him; people don't come and live where nobody knows them, for nothing," observed Mrs. Mary Smith.

"I dare say," returned the post-mistress, "Williams is not his real name."

"I don't know that," interrupted the landlady; "Williams is a good hanging name: there was Williams who murdered the Marr's family, and Williams who burked all those poor dear children; I dare say he is some relation of theirs; but to think of his coming to the White Hart—it's no place for his doings, I can tell him: he sha'n't poison his wife in my house; out he goes this very night—I'll take the letter to him myself."

"Lord! Lord! I shall be ruined, if it comes to be known that we take a look into the letters;" and the post-mistress thought in her heart that she had better let Mr. Williams poison his wife at his leisure. Mrs. Mary Smith, too, reprobated any violent measures; the truth is, she did not wish to be mixed up in the matter; a gentlewoman with an annuity and a front and back parlour was rather ashamed of being detected in such close intimacy with the post-mistress and the landlady. It seemed likely that poor Mrs. Williams would be left to her miserable fate.

"Murder will out," said the landlord, the following morning, as he mounted the piebald pony, which, like Tom Tough, had seen a deal of service; and hurried off in search of Mr. Crampton, the nearest magistrate.

Their perceptions assisted by brandy and water, he and his wife had sat up long past "the witching hour of night," deliberating on what line of conduct would be most efficacious in preserving the life of the unfortunate Mrs. Williams; and the result of their deliberation was to fetch the justice, and have the delinquent taken into custody at the very dinner table which was intended to be the scene of his crime.

"He has ordered soup to-day for the first time; he thinks he could so easily slip poison into the liquid. There he goes; he looks like a man who has got something on his conscience," pointing to Mr. Williams, who was walking up and down at his usual slow pace. Two o'clock arrived, and with it a hack chaise: out of it stept, sure enough, a lady and gentleman. The landlady's pity redoubled—such a pretty young creature, not above nineteen!—"I see how it is," thought she, "the old wretch is jealous." All efforts to catch her eye were in vain, the dinner was ready, and down they sat. The hostess of the White Hart looked alternately out of the window, like sister Ann, to see if any one was coming, and at the table to see that nothing was doing. To her dismay she observed the young lady lifting a spoonful of broth to her mouth! She could restrain herself no longer; but catching her hand, exclaimed, "Poor dear innocent, the soup is poisoned!"-All started from the table in confusion, which was yet to be increased:—a bustle was heard in the passage, in rushed a whole party, two of whom, each catching an arm of Mr. Williams, pinioned them down to his seat. "I am happy, madam," said the little bustling magistrate, "to have been under Heaven the humble instrument of preserving your life from the nefarious designs of that disgrace to humanity." Mr. Crampton paused in consequence of three wants—want of words, breath, and ideas.

"My life!" ejaculated the astonished lady.

"Yes, madam, the ways of Providence are inscrutable—the vain curiosity of three idle women has been turned to good account." And the eloquent magistrate proceeded to detail the process of inspection to which the fatal letter had been subjected; but when he came to the terrible words—"We will settle the matter to-morrow at dinner; but I am sorry you persist in poisoning your wife"—he was interrupted by bursts of laughter from the gentleman, from the injured wife, and even from the prisoner himself. One fit of merriment was followed by another, till it became contagious, and the very constables began to laugh too.

"I can explain all," at last interrupted the visitor. "Mr. Williams came here for that quiet so necessary for the labours of genius: he is writing a melodrame called 'My Wife'—he submitted the last act to me, and I rather objected to the poisoning of the heroine. This young lady is my daughter, and we are on our way to the sea-coast. Mr. Williams is only wedded to the Muses."

The disconcerted magistrate shook his head, and muttered something about theatres being very immoral.

"Quite mistaken, sir," said Mr. Williams. "Our soup is cold; but our worthy landlady roasts fowls to a turn—we will have them and the veal cutlets up—you will stay and dine with us—and, afterward, I shall be proud to read 'My Wife' aloud, in the hope of your approval, at least, of your indulgence"—and with the same hope, I bid farewell to my readers.

GIULIETTA—A TALE OF THE FOURTEENTH CENTURY

The crimson shadows of the evening, mantling over the sky, and mirrored on the ocean, steeping the marble villas on the coast with their rich hues, and giving the pale orange-flowers a blush not their own—how welcome were they after a day so sultry as that which had just set over Genoa! The sea-breeze came fresh, as if its wings were cool with sweeping over snowy mountains, or those islands of ice of which northern voyagers tell, but softened ere it reached the land by thousand odours which floated from the shore.

But there was one eye to which the glad sunset brought no light, one lip to which the evening wind brought no freshness, though the heavy arm-chair had been drawn to the window, and the lattice flung back to its utmost extent. The Lady Giulietta Aldobrandini was far beyond their gentle influences; yet a few more nights, and hers would be the deep, unbroken sleep of death. It was hard to die, with such ties as bound her to life. She gazed on the three lovely girls, who watched her lightest look, and felt how

bitter it was to know that in a few more days they would be motherless: she had supplied their father's loss, but who could supply hers? She had been commending them to the care of their uncle, the Cardinal Aldobrandini, who had undertaken the charge of those who would so soon be orphans; but her heart yearned to say yet more, and she signed to them to leave the room. The cardinal watched with moistened eyes their graceful figures disappear amid the shower of scented leaves, which, as they passed, they shook from the flowering shrubs, and his lip quivered as he said, "And how may I supply a mother's place to those most ill-fated children? Is there no hope, Giulietta?" and, even as he spoke, his own conviction answered, "There is none."

The countess replied not to his question touching herself. She knew that it was asked in vain, and she had yet much to say. "Two of them will cumber you but little; Constanza and Bianca are of calm and gentle natures; from infancy they have felt sorrow lightly, and their affection is half habit. I feel within my dying soul a stedfast conviction that life to them will be as an unbroken stream, whose tranquil course no fierce wind has ever ruffled. But, my name-child, my Giulietta, she, whose eyes fill with tears, and whose cheek reddens at the slightest emotion, whose strong feelings and whose timid temper require at once so much caution and yet so much encouragement—for Giulietta's future I tremble. God forgive me, if my youngest has been my dearest! but they have not known it; I knew it not myself till now."

She sank back exhausted; and for a moment Aldobrandini was too much moved to reply. He was a man in whom all earthly affections were reputed to be dead. Cold and stern in manner, rigid in conduct, severe in judgment, he knew no interests but those of the church which he served. His talents were great, and his influence in Genoa almost unbounded; for his bitterest foe—and the successful have always enemies—had no hold on a man who had no weaknesses. But, where the desert seems most bare, be sure the sun has burned most fiercely; and the young and enthusiastic Giulio Aldobrandini had given little indication of the future cold and impassive prelate. He was the younger son, and the beautiful Giulietta was the betrothed of his brother. It was said that the bride looked somewhat pale, and it was deemed a harsh decree which had sent the younger Aldobrandini to a distant convent. Time passed as rapidly as time ever passes, be the change what it will upon its path; and when Aldobrandini returned to his native city, he looked wan and worn, but it was with toil and vigil that had brought their own reward: for, in those days, ability and energy found a ready career to power and honour in the church. It may be believed that Aldobrandini would not have exchanged the waking certainties of his ambition for the realization of all his once—romantic fantasies; but, for a moment, the flood of years rolled back, the woman he had once so loved was dying at his side, and feeling became but the more bitter from the consciousness of the vanity of indulgence.

"Giulietta," at length, he said, in a low and broken tone, "years have passed since you and I spoke of the future as of a thing in which we took interest together. Then we spoke in vain: not so now; for, let the remembrance of our own youth be the pledge how precious another—your—Giulietta shall be in my sight."

The countess extended her emaciated hand towards him. Aldobrandini remembered it when its perfect beauty had been a model for the sculptor; he took it tenderly. Could it be the rigid and ascetic priest whose tears fell heavily on the dying Giulietta's hand? The lady was the first to recover her self. "Aldobrandini," she whispered, "I trust her happiness wholly to you." The girls now re-appeared in the garden, the cardinal himself beckoned them in, and, with a few brief but kind words, took his departure to the city.

Deeper and deeper fell the shades of melancholy over that sea-side villa. Day by day, those youthful sisters became more conscious of the approach of death. Their voices took a lower tone; their steps were more subdued; and their laughter, once so frequent, was unheard. At length, the worn eyes of the countess closed for ever: but their latest look was on her children.

Drearily did the rest of the summer pass away; and, when the leaves fell from the garden, and the bleak sea-breeze swept through the desolate lattices, it was with a feeling of rejoicing that the two elder sisters heard that they were to leave the villa, and pass the next year in the convent of Santa Caterina: after which their home would be the palace of the cardinal. But Giulietta left her mother's late dwelling with reluctance: it seemed almost like another separation. She visited and re-visited every spot which she could remember that the countess had once loved, and parted from it with many and bitter tears, as if it had been an animate object conscious of her regret. But youth is as a flowing stream, on whose current the shadow may rest but not remain; sunshine is natural to its glad waters, and the flowers will spring up on its banks: thus, though still preserving the most tender recollection of the parent whom she had lost, Giulietta's spirits gradually recovered their tone, and some very happy hours were spent in the convent.

A year in youth is like a month in spring; it is wonderful what an alteration it makes; the germ expands into a leaf, and the bud into a flower, almost before we have marked the change. On the cardinal's return from Rome, where he had made a long sojourn, he was surprised to perceive how the three Aldobrandini had sprung up into graceful womanhood. Constanza, the eldest, was nineteen, and Giulietta seventeen; but the sisters had never been parted, and he resolved that they should together take up their residence in his palace.

It was early in a spring evening when the Aldobrandini arrived at their uncle's dwelling. It was an old and heavy-looking building. Constanza and Bianca, as the massy gate swung behind them, on their arrival in the dark, arched court, simply remarked that they were afraid it would be very dull: but Giulietta's imagination was powerfully impressed; a vague terror filled her mind, which the gloom of the huge and still chambers through which they were ushered did not tend to decrease. At length, they paused in a large vaulted room, while the aged domestic went on, to announce them to the cardinal. Giulietta glanced around; the purple hangings were nearly black with age, so was the furniture, while the narrow windows admitted shadows rather than light. Some portraits hung on the walls, all dignitaries of the church; but the colour of their scarlet robes had faded with time, and each wan and harsh face seemed to turn frowning on the youthful strangers. A door opened, and they were ushered into the presence of their uncle. He was standing by a table, on which was a crucifix and an open breviary, while a volume of the life of St. Chrysostom lay open on the floor. A window of stained glass was half screened by a heavy curtain, and the dark panels of carved oak added to the gloom of the oratory. The sisters knelt before him, while gravely and calmly he pronounced over them a welcome and a blessing. Constanza and Bianca received them gracefully and meekly, but Giulietta's heart was too full; she thought how different would have been the meeting had they been but kneeling before parents instead of the stern prelate. She bowed her head upon the breviary; and her dark hair fell over her face while she gave way to a passionate burst of tears. Next to indulging in the outward expression of feeling himself, the cardinal held it wrong to encourage it in another. Gently, but coldly, he raised the weeping Giulietta; and, with kind but measured assurances of his regard and protection, he dismissed the sisters to their apartments. Could Giulietta have known the many anxious thoughts that followed her, how little would she have doubted her uncle's affection!

The light of a few dim stars shed a variable gleam amid the thick boughs of a laurel grove, too faint to mark the objects distinctly, but enough to guide the steps of one who knew the place. The air was soft and warm, while its sweetness told of the near growth of roses; but a sweeter breath than even the rose was upon the air, the low and musical whisper of youth and of love. Gradually, two graceful forms became outlined on the dark air—the one a noble-looking cavalier, the other Giulietta. Yet the brow of the cavalier was a gloomy one to turn on so fair a listener in so sweet a night; and his tone was even more sad than tender.

"I see no hope but in yourself. Do you think my father will give up his life's hatred to the name of Aldobrandini, because his son loves one of its daughters, and wears a sad brow for a forbidden bride? or, think you, that yonder stern cardinal will give up the plans and power of many years, and yield to a haughty and hereditary foe, for the sake of tears even in thy eyes, Giulietta?"

"I know not what I hope," replied the maiden, in a mournful, but firm voice; "but this I know, I will not fly in disobedience and in secrecy from a home which has been even as my own."

"And what," exclaimed the cavalier, "can you find to love in your severe and repelling uncle?"

"Not severe, not repelling, to me. I once thought him so; but it was only to feel the more the kindness which changed his very nature towards us. My uncle resembles the impression produced on me by his palace: when I first entered, the stillness, the time-worn hangings, the huge, dark rooms, chilled my very heart. We went from these old gloomy apartments to those destined for us, so light, so cheerful, where every care had been bestowed, every luxury lavished; and I said within myself, 'My uncle must love us, or he would never be thus anxious for our pleasure.' "

A few moments more, and their brief conference was over. But they parted to meet again; and at length Giulietta fled to be the bride of Lorenzo da Carrara. But she fled with a sad heart and tearful eyes; and when, after her marriage, every prayer for pardon was rejected by the cardinal, Giulietta wept as if such sorrow had not been foreseen. Her uncle felt her flight most bitterly. He had watched his favourite niece, if not with tenderness of look and tone, yet with deep tenderness of heart. When her elder sisters married and left his roof, he missed them not: but now it was a sweet music that had suddenly ceased, a soft light that had vanished. The only flower that, during his severe existence, he had permitted himself to cherish, had passed away even from the hand that sheltered it. It was an illusion fresh from

his youth: his love for the mother had revived in a gentler and holier form for her child, and now that, too, must perish. He felt as if punished for a weakness; and all Giulietta's supplications were rejected: for pride made his anger seem principle. "I have been once deceived," said he; "it will be my own fault if I am deceived again."

Yet how tenderly was his kindness remembered, how bitterly was his indignation deplored, by the youthful Countess da Carrara!—for such she now was—Lorenzo's father having died suddenly, soon after their union. The period of mourning was a relief; for bridal pomp and gaiety would have seemed too like a mockery, while thus unforgiven and unblessed by one who had been as a father in his care. At her earnest wish they fixed their first residence in the marine villa where her mother died.

"And shall you not be sad, my Giulietta?" asked her husband. "Methinks the memory of the dead is but a mournful welcome to our home."

"Tender, not mournful," said she. "I do believe that even now my mother watches over her child, and every prayer she once breathed, every precept she once taught, will come more freshly home to my heart, when each place recalls some word or some look there heard and there watched. It is for your sake, Lorenzo, I would be like my mother."

They went to that fair villa by the sea; and pleasantly did many a morn pass in the large hall, on whose frescoed walls was painted the story of Œnone, she whom the Trojan prince left, only to return and die at her feet. On the balustrade were placed sweet-scented shrubs, and marble vases filled with gathered flowers; and, in the midst, a fountain, whose spars and coral seemed the spoil of some sea-nymph's grotto, fell down in a sparkling shower, and echoed the music of Giulietta's lute. Pleasant, too, was it in an evening to walk the broad terrace which overlooked the ocean, and watch the silver moonlight reflected on the sea, till air and water were but as one bright element.

And soon had Carrara reason to rejoice that he had yielded to his wife's wish; for, ere they had been married three months, the plague broke out in Genoa, with such virulence as if, indeed, a demon had been unchained upon earth. "The spirit of your mother, my sweet wife, has indeed been our guardian angel," said the count, as he watched a fresh sea-breeze lift up the long dark curls, and call the crimson into Giulietta's cheek. Still, though safe themselves—for, though the distance from Genoa was but short, their secluded situation and the sea-air precluded all fear of infection—still an atmosphere of terror and woe was around them, and their thoughts were carried out of their own sweet home by dim and half-told tales of the dangers around them. And, among other things, Giulietta heard of her uncle's heroic conduct; others fled from the devoted city—but he fled not; others shut themselves up in their lonely palaces—he went forth amid the dead and dying; his voice gave consolation to the sick man, and his prayer called on Heaven for mercy to the departed soul. Giulietta heard, and in the silence of her chamber wept; and, when her tears were done, knelt, and gave thanks to God for her uncle.

For the first time hope arose within her, and she said to herself—"He who walks now even as an angel among his fellow-men cannot but forgive the errors and the weakness of earth. She went to meet her husband with a lightened heart; but, as she met him on the terrace, she saw that his brow was clouded, and his first words told her that important business would oblige him to go for a week to an ancient castle on the verge of the state, as his neighbours were disposed to question his boundary rights. It was but a day's, a summer day's, journey, through a healthy district; and yet how sorrowful was the parting! Alas! how soon the presence of beloved ones becomes a habit and a necessity! but a few weeks with them at our side, and we marvel however life was endured without them. The young countess touched her lute—it had no music; she gathered flowers—they had no sweetness; she turned to the fairy page of Ariosto—but she took no interest in his knights or dames; and at length the day was spent ere she had finished pacing the hall, and imagining all the possible and impossible dangers that could befall Carrara.

She was walking languidly on the terrace early the following morning, when a hum of voices caught her ear; one name rivetted her attention: a horrible conviction rushed upon her mind. She called a page, who at first equivocated: but the truth was at last owned. The cardinal was stricken with the plague. She signed to the page to leave her, and sank for a moment against one of the columns. It was but for a moment. She withdrew her hands from her face: it was pale, but tearless; and she left the terrace for her chamber with a slow but firm step. Two hours afterwards, the countess was sought by her attendants, but in vain; a letter was found addressed to their master, and fastened by one long, shining curl of raven darkness, which all knew to be hers.

Leaving the household to the dismay and confusion which such a departure occasioned, we will follow the steps of the countess, who was now on the road to Genoa. She had waited but to resume the black serge dress, which, as a novice of St. Caterina's, she had worn, and in which she knew she might pass

for one of the sisters who had vowed attendance on the sick; and, during the hour of the siesta, made her escape unobserved. Giulietta had been from infancy accustomed to long rambles by the sea-shore, or through the deep pine-forests; but now, though her purpose gave her strength, she felt sadly weary; when, on the almost deserted road, she overtook a man who was driving a small cart laden with fruit and vegetables. She accosted him; and the offer of a few piastres at once procured a conveyance to Genoa, for thither was her companion bound.

"The plague," said he, "makes every thing so scarce, that my garden has brought me a little fortune; it is an ill wind that blows nobody good."

"And are you not afraid of the infection?" asked the seeming Sister of Charity.

"Nothing hazard nothing win. A good lining of ducats is the best remedy for the plague," returned the gardener.

"Holy Madonna," thought Giulietta, "shall I not encounter for gratitude and dear love the peril which this man risks for a few ducats!"

The quarter where stood her uncle's palace was at the entrance of the city, and to reach it they had to traverse the principal street. How changed since last the countess passed that way! Then it was crowded with gay equipages and gayer company. She remembered the six white mules with their golden trappings, which drew the emblazoned coach of her uncle along; and how she leant back upon its purple velvet cushions, scarcely daring to glance amid the crowd of white-plumed cavaliers who reined in the curvettings of their brave steeds, lest she should meet Lorenzo da Carrara's eye, and betray their whole secret in a blush. Now not one living creature walked the street, and the sound of their light cart was like thunder. She was roused from her reverie by observing that her companion was taking an opposite direction to that of the palace; and requested to alight, mentioning her destination.

"To the archbishop's! Why, you will not find one living creature there. The good cardinal would have all the sick he could find brought to his palace, but they fell off like dried leave; and when he was struck with the plague himself none ventured to approach it; for we all agree that the air there must be more deadly than elsewhere, since it has not even spared his eminence. So, if it is there you are bound, Madonna, we part company; but it is just tempting Providence."

Giulietta's only answer was to offer the gardener a small sum for her conveyance; but to her surprise he refused it. "No, no, you are going on a holier errand than I; keep your money; you will want it all if you stay in this city, every thing is so dear."

A sudden thought struck Giulietta. "I do not ask you," said she, "to venture to a spot which seems marked for destruction; but if I meet you here to-morrow will you bring with you a small supply of provisions and fruit? I can afford to pay for them."

"I will come, be sure," replied the man; "and the saints keep you, maiden, for your errand is a perilous one. He watched her progress till she disappeared round a corner in the street. "I wish," muttered he, "I had gone with her to the palace; at all events, I will be here to-morrow; she is, for all her black veil and pale face, so like my little Minetta. Ay, ay, if this plague lasts, I shall be able to tell down her dowry in gold;" and the gardener pursued his way.

When Giulietta arrived at her uncle's palace, she paused for a moment, not in fear but in awe, the stillness was so profound; not one familiar sound broke upon her ear. The doors were all open, and she entered the hall; pallets were ranged on each side, and on one or two of the small tables stood cups and phials; but not a trace appeared of an habitant. On she passed through the gloomy rooms; everything was in disorder and out of place: it was indeed as if a multitude had there suddenly taken up their abode and as suddenly departed. But Giulietta hurried on to her uncle's sleeping apartment; it was vacant. Her heart for the first time sank within her, and she leant against the wain scot, sick and faint. "I have yet a hope," exclaimed she, and even as she spoke she turned to seek the oratory. She was right. The crucifix stood, and the breviary was open on the small table, even as they were the first time she entered that room: and on a rude mattress beside it lay her uncle. She sank on her knees, for he lay motionless; but, thanks to the holy Virgin, not breathless; no, as she bent over him, and her lips touched his, she could perceive the breath, the precious breath, of life: his hand too! it burnt in hers, but she could feel the pulse distinctly.

Giulietta rose, and threw herself before the crucifix. A violent burst of tears, the first she had shed, relieved her; and then calmly she prayed aloud for strength to go through the task which she had undertaken. The room was hot and oppressive; but she opened the window, and the sweet air came in, fresh and reviving from the garden below. She bathed her uncle's temples with aromatic waters, and poured into his mouth a few drops of medicine. He opened his eyes, and turned faintly on his pallet, but sank back, as though exhausted. Again he stretched out his hand, as if in search for something, which failing to find he moaned heavily. Giulietta perceived at once that parching thirst was consuming him. From the balcony a flight of steps led to the garden; she flew down them to the fountain, whose pure, cold water made the shadow of the surrounding acacias musical as ever. She returned with a full pitcher; and the eagerness with which the patient drank told how much that draught had been desired. The cardinal raised his head, but was quite unconscious; and all that long and fearful night had Giulietta to listen to the melancholy complainings of delirium.

The next day, she went to meet the gardener, who had waited, though, as he owned, in hopelessness of her coming. How forcibly the sense of the city's desolation rose before Giulietta, when she remembered that her ignorance of the hour proceeded from there being no one now to wind up the church-clocks! Again she returned to the unconscious sufferer; but little needs it to dwell on the anxiety or the exertion in which the next three days were passed. On the early morning of the last, as she watched over her uncle's pillow, she perceived that there was a slight moisture on his skin, and that his sleep was sound and untroubled. His slumbers were long and refreshing; and when he awoke it was with perfect consciousness. Dreading the effect of agitation, Giulietta drew her veil over her face, and to his enquiry of 'was any one there?' she answered in a low and feigned voice.

"I am faint and want food; but who, daughter, are you, who thus venture into the chamber of sickness and death?"

"A stranger; but one whose vow is atonement."

"Giulietta!" exclaimed the cardinal, and the next moment she was at his side; and both wept the sweetest tears ever shed by affection and forgiveness. Eagerly she prepared for him a small portion of food, and then, exerting the authority of a nurse, for bade all further discourse, and, soon exhausted, he slept again.

The cool shadows of the coming evening fell on the casement, when Giulietta first ventured to propose that she should send a letter by the gardener to Lorenzo, and desire that a litter might be sent to convey her uncle to their villa.

"My sweet child, do with me as you will," said the cardinal; "take me even to the house of a Carrara."

"And nowhere could you be so welcome," said a stranger entering, and Giulietta, springing from her knees, found herself in the arms of her husband. "I knew, Giulietta, I should find you here, though your letter told me but of prayer and pilgrimage."

And what now remains to be told? The cardinal accompanied them to the villa, where his recovery was rapid and complete: and the deep love which he witnessed in that youthful pair made him truly feel how great had been Giulietta's devotion to himself. The plague had done its worst in Genoa; and men were enabled to return to their habits, their occupations, and their duties, things ever inseparably connected. The plague had done its worst in Genoa; and men were enabled to return to their habits, their occupations, and their duties, things ever inseparably connected. The[1] cardinal from that hour treated Lorenzo da Carrara as a son; and their family union was happy as self-sacrifice and enduring affection could make it. In the picture-gallery, there is still preserved a portrait of the countess in her novice's garb; her cheek pale, her graceful form hidden by the black serge robe, and her beautiful hair put out of sight; and the count, her husband, used to say that "she never looked more lovely."

THE ENCHANTRESS

Water—the mighty, the pure, the beautiful, the unfathomable—where is thy element so glorious as it is in thine own domain, the deep seas? What an infinity of power is in the far Atlantic, the boundary of two separate worlds, apart like those of memory and of hope! or in the bright Pacific, whose tides are turned to gold by a southern sun, and in whose bosom sleep a thousand isles, each covered with the verdure, the flowers, and the fruit of Eden! But, amid all thy hereditary kingdoms, to which hast thou given beauty, as a birthright, lavishly as thou hast to thy favourite Mediterranean? The silence of a summer night is now sleeping on its bosom, where the bright stars are mirrored, as if in its depths they had another home and another heaven. A spirit, cleaving air midway between the two, might have paused to ask which was sea, and which was sky. The shadows of earth and earthly things, resting omen-like upon the waters, alone shewed which was the home and which the mirror of the celestial host.

But the distant planets were not the only lights reflected from the sea; an illuminated villa, upon the extreme point of a small rising on the coast, flung down a flood of radiance from a thousand lamps. From the terrace came the breath of the orange-plants, whose white flowers were turned to silver in the light which fell on them from the windows. Within the halls were assembled the fairest and noblest of Sicily.

Everyone, they say, has a genius for something—that of Count Arezzi was for festivals. A king, or more, the Athenian Pericles, might have welcomed his most favoured guests in such a chamber. The walls were painted in fresco, as artists paint whose present is a dream of beauty, and whose future is an immortality. Each fresco was a scene in Arcadia; and the nymphs, who were there gathering their harvest of roses, were only less lovely than the Sicilian maidens that flitted past. Among these was one much darker than her companions; her Eastern mother had bequeathed to her her black hair and her olive skin; in her eye was that brightness, and on her cheek was that freshness, which belong only to the earliest hour of youth—the blush had been too fleeting to burn, the smile too clear to cast that shadow which even light flings as it lengthens. But to-night the colour was heightened, the eyes wore a deeper shade, for the hue of the downcast lash was upon them, and the sweet half-opened mouth was too earnest for a smile.

Lolah was listening to those charmed words which change the girl at once into the woman—we step not over the threshold of childhood till led by Love. Alas, this knowledge is almost always heralded by a sorrow! That morning had Lolah heard from her stern uncle, that the love she bore to her cousin Leoni di Montefiore was a childish toy, and as such was to be put away; and all her happiness had been destroyed by having to reflect upon it. Poor Lolah! how hard it is to teach the young that life is made up of many parts; and that wealth, rank, power, are more to be desired than affection! To-night she was listening to Leoni—and who ever thought of the future when the present has first taught us we love and are beloved?—still, her eyes were filled with tears, and her heart beat heavier than usual. Leoni spoke of hope; but is not hope only a more gentle word for fear? And yet, with that mysterious contradiction which makes the fever of human existence, neither would have renounced the certainty of the other's affection for the careless content of yesterday. Strange, that ignorance should be our best happiness in this life, and yet be the one we are ever striving to destroy!

Leoni and his cousin stood in one of the deep windows; she leaning as if to inhale the fragrance of an Indian rose, and mark a flower which, brought from a far land, seemed more delicate than its bright companion. A pedestal of the green malachite stood beside, and on it a vase carved with the sacrifice of Iphigenia; these shut them out from the rest of the dancers.

"My father," exclaimed Leoni, "gave his daughter to her father;"—then a bitter thought of the wasted heritage, which had made his noble name a fetter rather than an aid, for a moment caused the lover to pause.

"Holy Mother!—but my uncle has just entered the room; let me go, ere he finds me talking to you."

Lolah waited not for an answer; another moment, and she had passed her slender arm through that of one of her companions, and was lost in the crowd. It was so sudden, Leoni scarcely believed she was gone: surely her sweet low sigh was on the air—no! it was but the breath of the Bengal rose. His eye wandered round; it fell on the sculptured vase, and there stood the Grecian father, a witness to the sacrifice of his youngest and loveliest child.

"Even so, my gentle Lolah, will the altar be thy tomb."

Leoni started, for a figure now stepped from the shade of the column: not only his last words, but their whole conversation must have been heard.

"Yes, Don Leoni," said the intruder, replying rather to his thoughts and look, "I have heard your discourse; pardon me when I say it was wilfully overheard. It is long since I have hearkened to the eager and happy words of young affection, and I listened as if to music; and, like music, they have died in hearing."

Leoni thought he would as soon that the dialogue had not been quite so attractive—strange, that it should be so to the cold and proud Donna Medora!

Again his companion answered to his thoughts—"You marvel at my speech; I could wonder myself at this still lingering sympathy with the base lot of humanity: but mortal breath and mortal frame cannot quite break away from mortal ties. Don Leoni, I pity you—I wish to serve you: I know not, if in giving you wealth I give you happiness; but wealth I can give. This is not the place for such words as mine must be. Breathe not in living ear what I have said: my power to serve you depends on your silence. Come to-morrow to our palazzo."

Medora turned from him, and descended the terrace. The weakness of our nature—how soon any strong emotion masters it! Leoni stood breathless with surprise and hope; he had once or twice before seen Donna Medora, and he had heard much of her. Young—she had seen but three-and-twenty summers deepen into autumn; beautiful—for it was as if Heaven had set its seal on her perfect face,— her life was one of sadness and solitude. The cathedral where she knelt, the poor whom she aided, the sick-room of her aged father, and her own lonely chamber—these were the haunts of Medora. When about seventeen, a severe illness had stricken her even unto death; almost by a miracle she was restored to life, but never to youth—the shadow of the grave, to which she had so nearly approached, seemed to rest upon her. Her glad laugh never again made the air musical as with the singing of a bird in spring; her light step forgot the dance; and her lute was given to another. The sympathy she once had for joy was now kept entire for sorrow; but the mother who died in her arms, the father whose long and sickly age she soothed and supported, thought her nature had, in so nearly approaching heaven, caught something of its elements. And Lolah, who, as a distant relative, sometimes visited Don Manfredi's chamber, said that Medora was almost an angel; and added—"I should think her quite one, but that I do not fear her, and that she seems unhappy."

It was reported that love and religion had held a bitter conflict in her heart. Before her illness she had been betrothed to a young cavalier; on her recovery she refused to fulfil her engagement, alleging that the instability of life had taught her the vanity of human ties: all she now asked, was to devote what remained of existence to her aged parents. Remonstrances, prayers, were alike unavailing; and the young Count Rivoli became one of the Knights of Malta. Some years had since passed; and in the gay and hurrying circle of Palermo, Medora's name was rarely mentioned.

Leoni dwelt upon her promise of assistance; but the more he reflected, the more hopeless it seemed. How could she give wealth, the daughter of one of Sicily's poorest nobles?

Our young Sicilian was naturally of a daring and reckless temper; and resolving to hope, without analysing why or wherefore, he re-entered the saloon. He danced no more with Lolah; yet he had the satisfaction of seeing her look sad and languid while dancing with another. But how restless was the night that followed! Hope is feverish enough at all times; what must it be when stimulated by curiosity!

The first blush of morning awakened Leoni from his light slumbers: he looked out; the hue of the sky was that too of the sea; the waves of the Mediterranean floated on as if freighted with roses; yet how Leoni wished they were glittering with the clear colourless light of noon! Never say that time is of equal length: the movement of the hours is as irregular as the beating of the heart which measures them. A year of ordinary life, if counted by hopes, fears, and fancies, was in that lingering morning. At length, noon sounded from many a turret; and, regardless of the heat, the young Count hurried to the palazzo.

When he reached the pier, a crowd of boatmen offered their services.

"What, ho! Michele and Stefano! I have tried the swiftness of the Santa Catharina before now. Remember, I am as impatient as . . . ."

"Your lordship always is," replied Stefano, who, having an answer always ready, always answered.

Leoni jumped into the boat, whose celerity shewed that the wax taper her pious rowers offered to Santa Catherina yearly on the day of her fête, was not thrown away; though, perhaps, the activity of the brothers who rowed did as much as their piety towards sending the little vessel swiftly through the waters.

"You want to land," said Michele, "at San Marco's steps?" turning the head of the boat to the accustomed landing-place.

The steps to which San Marco lent his name had been worth many a sequin to them; for the winding path to the left led to Lolah's villa.

"No, no," replied Leoni; "to the Nymph's Cove."

"Signor," returned Michele, "those steps lead only to Count Manfredi's garden."

"And it is thither I am going."

The boatmen exchanged looks of astonishment bordering on dismay, which was not diminished by the silence of the usually gay cavalier. Montefiore leant back in the boat: as the interview drew nigh, a feeling of fear—not fear, that was what none of his house had ever yet known—but of awe, stole over him. Many a mood had that morning passed through his mind; disbelief—but surely the sad seriousness of such a one as Donna Medora could never stoop to mockery!—then hope, like a sweet summer-shower, when dark clouds break away into sudden light—till all his thoughts fixed on one mysterious circumstance—that he was the only person who had seen her the preceding evening. The Count d'Arezzi himself was not aware that she had been among his guests.

While musing on the singularity of this, they arrived at the landing-place, and found the Senora's page in waiting. Dumb from his birth, the boy Julio had been brought up in the Manfredi family, where his weak frame and want of language had exempted him from all but the lightest tasks.

"What would the Senora Lolah say to this visit?" cried Stefano, the moment his master was out of hearing. "The lady Medora is beautiful as an angel; I marvel we never rowed cavalier hither before."

"We never have; but I have, and in an evil hour. Well had it been for my first master if he had never looked on a face so fair and so false. I remember when I was wont of an evening to row the Count Rivoli to this very spot. We used to see a white veil waving among the trees—it was the Senora watching his approach: they were very happy then. But I know not how it was, unless it be the inconstancy of women; for change is as natural to them as it is to the sea. The lady Medora was taken dangerously ill: during her fearful sickness, never was truer lover than my master; the shrine of Our Lady was laden with gifts; and night after night he paced beneath the window of her room,—till she who lay dying above, could scarcely look paler than he who watched below. And yet, on her recovery she refused to wed him. She declared, that, in her danger, she had made a vow not to marry. They say the young Count knelt at her feet, but in vain; and for her sake he forswore the face of woman and his native country. Count Rivoli is now a Knight of Malta. What has the Senora Medora to do with another lover?"

"Well, yonder gallant's step is not much like a lover's," replied Stefano, as a bend in the path enabled them to see the slow and thoughtful pace at which Leoni followed his guide.

The boy who led the way walked feebly and languidly, and Montefiore hurried him not. The gloom of the neglected garden added to that on his spirits; and the wild eyes and pale face of his dumb attendant seemed to fix his attention painfully. It was a countenance whose unhappiness was catching; for Leoni thought how terrible was his lot, debarred from that noblest privilege of humanity, interchange of thought, and its sweetest interchange of feelings! The boy stopped suddenly at the door of a summer-house, so hidden by the dark branches of the pine-trees around, that the stranger might have passed it by unnoticed. They entered together; the page approached his mistress, pointed to the visitor, and then left the room.

Without rising from her own seat, Medora signed to Leoni to take the one opposite. At first she seemed so absorbed in thought, that even his entrance was insufficient to rouse her; she evidently hesitated to speak, as if she had not yet resolved on the purport of her words. Her young and impetuous companion found the silence very oppressive; but even his impetuosity was subdued by the gloom around him.

Panelled with the scarce woods of other lands, whose cornices were carved in quaint wreaths of flowers, mingled with crosses of divers shapes and the family arms, it was obvious that a rich though barbarous taste had here once lavished its wealth. But Time had, as usual, laughed the works of man to scorn; and pomp amidst its decay sickened over its vanity. The colours were all merged in the heavy black of age; the gildings were tarnished; and the cornices broken and defaced. The temple, of which but a few fallen columns remain—the mighty city, whose stately fragments are strewed in the desert— are solemn, not sorrowful. But the desolation of yesterday comes home to every man's heart—to-morrow its portion may be his own; and the faded tapestry, the discoloured floor, and the mouldering painting, speak of sorrow which still exists, and poverty which is still endured.

Leoni gazed round the gloomy banquet-room, and remembered a festival which had been given there; he was a child at the time, and perhaps his memory lent something of its own gaiety to the scene. But he was roused from his revery by Medora's voice.

"My silence, Count," said she, "must seem strange; but when you have heard the story I am about to reveal, you will not marvel that I hesitate to speak words which are even as those of Fate. You love, and you are beloved; surely you might be happy. There is but one obstacle, that of wealth. Leoni, I can make you rich—rich as the fabled kings, who poured forth gold like water: dare you accept the offer?"

"On what conditions?" exclaimed Leoni, almost unconsciously clasping the cross of the order which hung at his neck.

"On none," returned his companion. "Fear not my conditions, but your own use of the wealth I can bestow. Dare you take your destiny into your own hands? But I will place my life before you, and then judge for yourself."

Medora rose from her seat.

"Not here, where the uncharmed air might bear away my words, dare I tell my history. Count Leoni, you have heard of wondrous and fearful secrets, whose spell is over stars and over spirits; you have heard of mortals to whom immortal power is given—such power is mine. You deem you are speaking to your cousin—would that you were! I have but the borrowed likeness of her whose life long since reached its appointed boundary. Give me your hand, and in a few minutes we shall be in my own dwelling, amid those immeasurable deserts where only my story may be communicated. Do you consent to accompany me?"

Leoni answered by taking the hand extended towards him. Even as he touched it, a vapour filled the room; he felt himself raised with a sudden and dizzy velocity; he leant back; the cloud was as the wave on which a swimmer floats, borne by no effort of his own; and a pleasant sensation of sleep came over him. He was roused by the light touch of his companion, and startled into consciousness. They were standing on the top of a mighty tower; one of those, whose height, seen from below, seems to reach even unto the heavens—but the summit once gained, we only find what an immeasurable upward distance remains. A hot, bright noon filled the air with light, but not with fertility; for far as the eye could reach—and the clear colourless atmosphere seemed to extend the sight even to infinity—spread an arid desert, as if sand were an element, and only shared its empire with the sky. But immediately around the tower lay the giant ruins of a once glorious city; one of those built when the world was in the strength of its youth, and reared buildings which were the work of centuries, and yet but the work of a life: the cradle and the grave were then far apart. Now the shadow of the last rests upon the first, and all life groans beneath the weight and darkness thereof. Then the marble of the quarry and the gold of the mine lay on the surface; the fertile soil of the East yielded forth its abundance; and the labour which was in man's destiny, needed not to be all given to that sad and perpetual strife with hunger which belongs to our worn-out and weary age.

It seemed, however, as if Time had long paused in his work of destruction; the vast masses of carved granite, the broken columns, the shattered walls where once four chariots drove abreast, all remained as they had done for ages. Year after year the burning sunshine forbade the rain to fall, and speedily dried up the dews of night; no green moss, no creeping plant, as in his native Italy, hid the ruin which they were aiding: the bare white marble shone distinct from the sands.

Leoni turned to his companion; her face and garb were wholly changed: she stood upon her native tower, and had resumed her native shape. As Medora, she had been so like his own Lolah—a slight, low figure, whose grace was that of childhood; the same sweet pleading eyes; alike, save that hope gave its gladness to the face of Leila, while that of Medora had all the mournfulness of memory. But the glorious beauty of the being at his side, though it wore the shape, had scarce the semblance of mortality. The face had that high and ideal cast of beauty which made the divinities of Greece divine; for the mind was embodied in the features. The large blue eyes were of the colour of the noon, when heaven is full of light; they looked upon you like the far-off shining of some vast and lonely planet. Her garb and turban had an Oriental splendour; a silver veil mingled with her rich profusion of hair, which was bound by strings of costly pearls. Round her arm was rolled a band of gold, and on her hand she bore a signet of some strange clear stone, covered with mystic characters. Her height and step were like a queen's, such as might have beseemed the young Empress of Palmyra, ere she walked in the triumph of the Roman conqueror.

"I may not enter," said she, "the hall of my father's tomb but in mine own shape: follow me."

Casting the golden sandals from her feet she led the way down a flight of black marble steps. They paused at the foot of the tower; two enormous doors flew open, and though it was the bright light of noon he had left behind, Leoni stood dazzled at the glory of the hall. The crystal roof was traversed by a shining zodiac, lit by a pale unearthly flame; the black marble floor was covered with inscriptions in gold, but they were in unknown ciphers: Leoni observed, however, that they were similar to those on the girdle and the border of his companion's robe. The gigantic pillars which supported the vast dome were also of black marble, covered, in like manner with golden hieroglyphics. Between them were immense vases, each one a varying mosaic of precious stones, and filled with the same pale flame which lighted the zodiac above. In the centre of the hall stood a huge crystal globe, and upon its summit a funeral urn of the purest alabaster, on which neither figure nor sign was graven. Around were placed seven silver tripods, whereon were burning odoriferous woods, which filled the air with their perfumes.

"In yonder urn," said Medora, "lie the ashes of my father. I have obtained that gift in search of which his life was spent; and yet I would that our mingled ashes were strewn on those elements we have mastered, and in vain."

She now seated herself on a radiant throne opposite, and Leoni leant on the lion's skin at her feet. We have said the Leoni was of a race to whom fear was unknown, yet he felt his heart beat quicker than ordinary, and his glance quailed before the melancholy and spiritual beauty of the eyes now shining upon him.

"You see in me," said his mysterious companion, "the only living descendant of those Eastern Magi to whom the stars revealed their mysteries, and spirits gave their power. Age after age did sages add to that knowledge which, by bequeathing to their posterity, they trusted would in time combat to conquer their mortality. But the glorious race perished from the earth, till only my father was left, and I his orphan child. Marvels and knowledge paid his life of fasting and study. All the spirits of the elements bowed down before him; but the future was still hidden from his eyes, and Death was omnipotent. His power of working evil had no bounds, but his power of good was limited; and yet it was good that he desired. How dared he put in motion those mighty changes, which seemed to promise such happiness on earth, while he was ignorant of what their results might be? and of what avail was the joy he might pour out on life, over whose next hour the grave might close, and only make the parting breath more bitter from the blessings which it was leaving behind?

"I was no unworthy daughter of such a sire; I advanced in these divine studies even to his wish, and looked to the future with a hope which many years had deadened in himself, but from which I caught an omen of ultimate success. Alas! he mastered not his destiny: I have said before, his ashes are in yonder urn. A few unwholesome dews on a summer night were mightier than all his science. For a time I struggled not with despair: but youth is buoyant, and habit is strong. Again I pored over the mystic scroll—again I called on the spirits with spell and with sign. Many a mystery was revealed, many a wonder grew familiar, but still Death remained at the end of all things, as before. One night I was on the terrace of my tower. Above me was the deep blue sky, with its stars—worlds filled, perchance, with the intelligence which I sought. On the desert below was the phantasm of a great city. I looked on its small and miserable streets, where hunger and cold reigned paramount, and man was a wretched as if flung but yesterday on the earth, and there had been as yet no time for art to yield its assistance, or labour to bring forth its fruit. I gazed next on scenes of festivity, but they were not glad; for I looked from the wreath into the head it encircled, and from the carcanet of gems to the heart which beat beneath—and I saw envy, and hate, and repining, and remorse. I turned my last glance on the palace within its walls; but there the purple was spread as a pall, and the voice of sorrow and the cry of pain were loud on the air. I bade the shadows roll away upon the winds, and rose depressed and in sorrow. I was not alone: one of those glorious spirits, whose sphere was far beyond the power of our science, whose existence we rather surmised than knew, stood beside me.

"From that hour a new existence opened before me. I loved, and I was beloved—love, to which imagination gave poetry, and mind gave strength, was the new element added to my being. Alas! how little do the miserable race to which I belong know of such a feeling! They blend a moment's vanity, a moment's gratification, into a temporary excitement, and they call it love. Such are the many, and the many make the wretchedness of earth. And yet your own heart, Leoni, and that of my gentle cousin, may witness for my words, there are such things as truth, and tenderness, and devotion in the world; and such redeem the darkness and degradation of its lot. Nay, more—if ever the mystery of our destiny be unravelled, and happiness be wrought out of wisdom, it will be the work of Love.

"It matters little to tell you of my blessedness; but my very heart was filled with the light of those radiant eyes, which were to me what the sun is to the world. Yet one dark shadow rested on my soul, beyond even their influence. Death had been the awful conqueror with whom my race had so often struggled, and to whom they had so often yielded. A mortal, I loved an immortal, and the fear of separation was ever before me; yet a long and a happy time passed away before my fear found words.

"It was one evening we were floating over the earth, and the crimson cloud on which we lay was the one where the sun's last look had rested. Its gleam fell on a small nook, while all around was fast melting into shade. Still, it was a sad spot which was thus brightened—it was a new-made grave. Over the others the long grass grew luxuriantly, and speckled, too, by many small and fragrant flowers; but on this, the dark-brown earth had been freshly turned up, and the red worm writhed restlessly about its disturbed habitation. Some roses had been scattered, but they were withered; their sweet leaves were already damp and discoloured. All wore the present and outward signs of our eternal doom—to perish in corruption.

"The shadows of the evening fell, deepening the gloom into darkness—the one last bright ray had long been past, when a youth came from the adjacent valley. That grave but yesterday received one who was to have been his bride—his betrothed from childhood for whose sake he had been to far lands and gathered much wealth, but who had pined in his absence and died. He flung himself on the loathsome place, and the night-wind bore around the ravings of his despair. Woe for that selfishness which belonged to my mortality! I felt at that moment more of terror than of pity. I thought of myself: Thus must I, with all my power, my science, and loved by one into whose sphere Death comes not, even thus must I perish! True, the rich spices, the perfumed woods, the fragrant oils, which would feed the sacred fire of my funeral pyre, would save my mortal remains from that corruption which makes the disgust of death even worse than its dread. A few odoriferous ashes along would be left for my urn. Yet not the less must I share the common doom of my race,—I must die!

"'Nay, my beautiful!' said the voice, which was to me as the fiat of life and death, so utterly did it fill my existence; why should we thus yield to a vague terror? Listen, my beloved! I know where the waters of the fountains of life roll their eternal waves—I know I can bear you thither and bid you drink from their source, and over lips so hallowed Death hath no longer dominion. But, alas! I know now what may be the punishment. Like yourselves, the knowledge of our race goes on increasing, and our experience, like your own, hath its agonies. None have dared what I am about to dare, and the future of my deed is even to me a secret. But what may not be borne for that draught which makes my loved one as immortal as my love?'

"I gazed on the glorious hope which lighted up his radiant brow, and I said to him, 'Give me an immortality which must be thine.' Worlds rolling on worlds lay beneath our feet when we stood beside the waters of life. A joyful pride swelled in my heart. I, the last and the weakest of my race, had won that prize which its heroes and its sages had found too mighty for their grasp. A sound as of a storm rushing over ocean startled me when I stooped to drink, the troubled waves rose into tumultuous eddies, their fiery billows parted, and from amid them appeared the dark and terrible Spirit of Necessity. The cloud of his awful face grew deeper as it turned on me. 'Child of a sinful and fallen kind!' said he, and he spoke the language most familiar to my ear, which yet sounded like that of another world, 'who have ever measured by their own small wisdom that which is infinite—drink, and be immortal! Be immortal, without the wisdom or the power belonging unto immortality. Drink!'

"I shrank from the starry waters as they rose to my lip, but a power stronger than my will compelled me to their taste. The draught ran through my veins like ice. Slowly I turned to where my once-worshipped lover was leaning. The same change had passed over both. Our eyes met, and each look into the other's heart, and there dwelt hate—bitter, loathing, and eternal hate. I had changed my nature; I was no longer the gentle, up-looking mortal he had loved. I had changed my nature; he was no longer to me the one glorious and adored being. We gazed on each other with fear and abhorrence. The dark power, whose awful brow was fixed upon us like Fate, again was shrouded in the kindling waters. By an impulse neither could control, the Spirit and I flung ourselves down the steep blue air, but apart, and each muttering, 'Never! never!' And that word 'never' told our destiny. Never could either feel again that sweet deceit of happiness, which, if it be a lie, is worth all truth. Never more could each heart be the world of the other.

"Our feelings are as little in our power as the bodily structure they animate. My love had been sudden, uncontrollable, and born out of my own will—and such was my hate. As little could I master the sick shudder his image now called up, as I could the passionate beating of the heart it had once excited. I stood alone in my solitary hall—I gazed on the eternal fire burning over the tomb of my father, and I wished it were burning over mine. For the first time I felt the limitations of humanity. The desire of my race was in me accomplished—I was immortal; and what was this immortality? A dark and measureless future. Alas, we had mistaken life for felicity! What was my knowledge? it only served to show its own vanity; what was my power, when its exercise only served to work out the decrees of an inexorable necessity? I had parted myself from my kind, but I had not acquired the nature of a spirit. I had lost of humanity but its illusions, and they alone are what render it supportable. The mystic scrolls over which I had once pored with such intenseness, were now flung aside; what could they teach me? Time was to me but one great vacancy; how could I fill it up, who had neither labour nor excitement? I sat me down mournfully, and thought of the past. Why, when love is perished, should its memory remain? I had said to myself, So long as I have life, one deep feeling must absorb my existence. A change—and that too of my own earnest seeking—had passed over my being; and the past, which had been so precious, was now as a frightful phantasm. The love which alters, in its inconstancy may set up a new idol, and worship again with a pleasant blindness; but the love which leaves the heart with a full knowledge of its own vanity and nothingness,—which saith, The object of my passion still remains, but it is worthless in my sight—never more can I renew my early feeling—I marvel how I ever could have loved—I loathe, I disdain the weakness in my former self;—ah, the end of such love is indeed despair!

"Do you mark yonder black marble slab, which is spread as over a tomb? It covers the most silvery fountain that ever mirrored the golden light of noon, or caught the fall of the evening dew, in an element bright as themselves. The radiant likeness of a Spirit rests on those waters. I bade him give duration to the shadow he flung upon the wave, that I might gaze on it during his absence. The first act of my immortality was to shut it from my sight. There must that black marble rest for ever.

"Why need I tell you of the desolation with which centuries have passed over my head? At length I resolved to leave my solitude, to visit earth; to seek, if I could not recall, my humanity; to interest myself in my species, and help even while I despised them. The thousand hues of sunset were deepening into the rich purple of twilight, when I passed over a Sicilian palace. Lemon and orange trees crowded the terrace, and their odours floated upwards towards an apartment where every casement was flung open for the sake of air. One emaciated hand stretched out on the purple silk coverlet, the other extended towards an aged female beside, reclined a young and beautiful girl; she was dying. A week of fever had done the work of years; life had burnt fiercely out; and the fragile tenement, wasted and worn away, lay in that languid repose which is the harbinger of death. The long black hair hung in pall-like masses; it had been loosened in the restlessness of pain. Her mother kept bathing the sunken temples with aromatics, but they throbbed no longer, and the sufferer motioned to her to desist. She now asked rest rather than relief; but life yet put forth its lasting energy in affection, and clasping her mother's hand, she turned her large soft eyes to her father. He stood watching her, as though, while he watched, life could not escape. Suddenly, a slight convulsion passed over the face of the dying girl; she gasped as if for air, and raised herself on her pillow without assistance, but sank back with the effort;—she was dead. A wild scream broke from the mother, and she fell senseless by the bed. The father caught the lifeless hands of his child, and, mad with despair, implored her not to leave him. Loud sobs came from the further part of the chamber: there was now no one to disturb by that passion of sorrow.

"Human misery is an awful sight. The old nurse approached the corse; she smoothed the long dark hair,—she placed a chaplet of roses on the brow, and a few fresh flowers in the lifeless hand. The rich light from the open casement fell on the white dress, and still whiter face, with a mocking cheerfulness. The aged creature could restrain her grief no longer; she rushed to a darker part of the room, and wept. A thought struck me: over the departed I had no power; but I could spare the agony of the living. Yes, I would take upon myself human relations, would bind myself by human ties,—I would be to them even as a daughter. The next moment I had assumed the shape of their child.

"Far in an unfrequented track of the southern seas lies a small island; there are aged trees and early blossoms; and amid them myriads of shining insects and bright-winged birds make the solitude glad with life; but they are its sole inhabitants. Once, driven away by a tempest from its ordinary course, a ship discovered the little isle. The Spaniards landed; they took possession in the name of the Madonna, and with pieces of grey rock piled up a cross. Human eye has never since dwelt on that lovely and lonely shore; but beneath the shadow of that cross lie the mortal remains of your cousin Medora,—Gradually I allowed some sign of returning life to appear; the old nurse, who was bending over the body, was the first to explain, 'Bring a looking-glass, for there is breath within those lips.' The slight cloud left on the mirror was as the very atmosphere of hope; eyes dim with weeping, cheeks pale with watching, were lighted up on the instant.

"I felt a new and keep happiness in the happiness I had given. It needs to tell how I gradually recovered, and how the parents, whose very life seemed bound up in their child's, were never weary of gazing on their recovered treasure. But a grief of which I had not dreamt awaited me. Medora had been betrothed to a young Sicilian nobleman. The moment an interview was permitted, the lover was at my feet, full of that hope and that joy he was never to know again. You are aware how the marriage was broken off, on the plea of a vow to the Virgin made in the extremity of danger; but you know now the agony I inflicted, or that I endured, in listening to the passionate despair of Rivoli; and when he said, 'Your death I might have borne—it was the will of God, and life would have lived on a hope beyond the grave, but thus to find you changed to me, to think that you can hold our love an offence in the sight of Heaven, and that I, who have loved, and who do love you so unutterably, that I should be the first sacrifice you offer up,— this, Medora, is more than I can bear!'

"In listening thus, how I repented me of my rash interference with the course of human life! If I had given joy, I had also caused more sorrow; and, worse, I had reason to question whether the grief of the marriage thus broken off did not embitter, despite of all my care, the brief period of Donna Maria's life.

"I have now little more to say of myself. The last few years have been devoted to Don Manfredi's declining age; wearisome has the task been, and still I have clung to it. I own, yet shun the fatal truth, that my lot is but an awful solitude, without duties or affections—those ties and blessings of humanity.—And now for the wealth I offer you; I know not its consequences, but I know those consequences can be but in your own acts. I do no more than a mere mortal might. On this interview there is imposed the condition—secrecy; on the possession of riches there is none. The spirits of riches are the first and the meanest which yield to science; it shall be my care that they reach you in simple and ordinary channels. Speak!"

"Give me," exclaimed Leoni, "give me wealth; give me Lolah!"

A purple cloud filled the glorious hall; again stupor overwhelmed him; again he awakened, and there he was in the lonely summer-room, and Medora, with her pale child-like face and black garments, at his side; but he met the large dark eyes filled with a strange wild light, and he knew it was no dream.

"Leave me now," said Medora; "but on your life be silent. Life and secrecy are one. Farewell!"

Dizzy with expectation, Leoni returned to the boat. The clock of San Francisco's abbey struck; he had been away but one hour. Pallid and abstracted, there was something in his look that effectually silence the boatmen; nay, they remained in gloomy stillness after he had left them.

"He has met with a refusal," at length said Stefano.

"Rather say, that there is evil in yon dreary palazzo and that pale girl, and their influence is on him. The lady Medora is kind and generous, but there is a curse follows her; and when did ever gift of hers turn to good?"

"The notary Signor Grazie awaits your pleasure," said a domestic, on Leoni's entrance to his palace.

The notary's business was soon told. The Marchese Ravenna, a distant relative of the young Count, had made him his heir; and boundless was the wealth the aged miser left behind him. That evening saw Leoni a welcome guest at his uncle's; and but a few weeks fled past, ere orange flowers bound the bridal tresses of his gentle cousin. The same day died Count Manfredi; and, as if her life were one with his, Donna Medora breathed her last at the very moment of her father's death.

"One, two, three; so late, so very late," exclaimed the Countess di Montefiore, "and Leoni still from home; there was a time when I dreamed not of keeping these solitary vigils."

Wearily Lolah arose from the velvet ottoman, and again the hour was struck by one of their own clocks, a few minutes later than the abbey; and it was succeeded (for the time-piece was a rare device of a skilful artist) by a sweet and lively air—one of those Neapolitan barcarolles which, like the glad music of Memnon's lyre, seemed inspired by the morning sunshine.

"Mockery," sighed the youthful watcher, "for the flight of time to be told in music!"

She began to pace the room,—that common resource of extreme lassitude, when sleep, to which the will consents not, hangs heavy on the eyelids. Truly, night was made for sleep; since to its wakeful hours belongs an oppression unknown to the very dreariest hours of day. The stillness is so deep, the solitude so unbroken, the fever brought on by want of rest so weakens the nerves, that the imagination exercises despotic and unwholesome power, till, if the heart have a fear or a sorrow, up it arises in all the force and terror of gigantic exaggeration.

The Countess had long since dismissed her attendants; yet the pearls still braided her hair, which hung nearly to her feet, in two large plaits; and a white silk robe, carelessly fastened at the waist, shrouding her whole figure in its loose folds, gave her something of that ghost-like appearance with which our fancy invests the habitants of another world. And truly, with her pale cheek and melancholy eyes, she looked like a spirit wandering mournfully around the scene of former pleasures. Yet what luxury was there not gathered in that gorgeous room? The purple silk curtains excluded the night-dews, while they allowed the air to enter freighted with odours from the orange-trees on the terrace below. The nuns of the Convent of St. Valerie, so celebrated for their skill in embroidery, had exerted their finest art in transferring all the flowers of spring to the white velvet ottomans: you might have asked, which was real—the rose on the cushion or that which hung from the crystal vase? The jewels lavished on the toys scattered round, had been held a noble dower by the fairest maiden in Sicily. On the walls were pictures, each one a world of thought and of beauty. The Grecian landscapes of Gaspar Poussin, who delighted in the graceful nymph, and the marble fane which recalled a mythology all poetry, as if in his dreams he had dwelt in Thessaly. The rugged scenes which Salvator Rosa loved to delineate—the forest, dark with impenetrable depths; the bare and jagged rock, rough as if nature had forgotten it; the aged pine riven by the lightning, and beside it some bandit, desolate and stricken as the tree by which he stood, but with a cruel defiance in his looks, as though he longed to resent all the injuries he had received from a few. Near at hand hung one of the glad earths and sunny skies in which the more buoyant spirit of Claude Lorraine revelled, as if its native element were sunshine. There were portraits too, the noble and the beautiful of her race; faces which told a whole history—and yet Lolah marked them not.

But one twelvemonth had she been a bride, and her husband's presence was unfamiliar to his home. Day after day did some unkind friend—for when do friends not delight in the sorrow of the prosperous?—come to her with tales how the Count's wealth was lavished on others less lovely than herself. And even that very evening had her father been with her, telling her that no wealth could hold out against Leoni's reckless prodigality—against his mad passion for gaming. In pity to the gentle creature, who could only lean on his bosom and weep, he might not tell her that the husband of her love was an object of universal suspicion, and that sorcery and the once stainless name of Montefiore were coupled together. He left her with those words of fondness which are never, and those words of comfort which ever are, said in vain. Wretched she had long been, but not till to-night had she owned the truth even to herself—owned that all her dreams of happiness, all the fairy creations of her fancy, had melted away, like the gardens and palaces she had seen painted on the air in the bay of Naples.

Weak, selfish, and vain, Leoni's was the very nature which wealth corrupts; he looked upon it but as the source of self-gratification. He forgot that the power with which the rich man is endued, is a sacred duty, whose neglect brings its own punishment; and that he who seeks pleasure with reference to himself, not others, will ever find that pleasure is only another name for discontent. At first Lolah was the idol of his heart—she became his bride—and a few happy weeks were passed in retirement and bliss; but Leoni soon looked beyond the small circle of the heart. They went to Palermo, and there he took delight in magnificence; his vanity exulted in glittering display, it was gratified by envy and wonder. Fête succeeded fête, till he himself grew weary of his prodigal hospitality: he craved for variety; and Lolah's timid and gentle temper was ill fitted to be the check he needed. Gambling soon became a habit; his enormous losses were an excitement; he knew he could repair them with a wish—he cared not, therefore, for the money he lost; but he desired to conquer fortune, and held success to be the triumph of skill. In the early part of his career, that evil and grudging feeling with which people regard great and sudden wealth, exhausted itself in prophecies of the certain ruin to which the young spendthrift Count was hastening; and when those prophecies were not fulfilled, their utterers were disappointed; they viewed it as a sin that he had proved their omens untrue. In sad truth, half our forebodings of our neighbours are but our own wishes, which we are ashamed to utter in any other form.

Gradually, the crowds at the Montefiore palace grew less noble; those whose consequence was diminished by its splendour, were the first to turn away; their example was followed by those who had nothing to gain; then went those who are ever led by example;—till the palace only gathered the dissipated and the dishonoured; the needy, who made want their plea, for even they needed an excuse; and the gamester, who was reckless whither he went, so that he indulged his passion. Old friends one after another became cold, and new friends were insolent and familiar. All this cut deep, and Leoni plunged still more madly into every possible excess; and when all other aids to forgetfulness failed, the red wine-cup was drained for oblivion.

Pale and sad the young Countess passed the weary hours in her splendid solitude; she felt the loss of friends less than Leoni, for had she not lost her husband? That evening had, however, been spent from home; it was the time of the Carnival—she had been to a masque as an Indian maiden; and now sat up for Leoni's return, half in girlish vanity, half because she could not bear the day to close without seeing him: she knew that he would let himself in by a private portal, which he had expressly made, and that he must cross that chamber on his way to his own. Chilly and fatigued, she again drew the rich flower-wrought cashmere around her; for a moment she sat, her cheek resting on her hand; at length she leaned back on the ottoman, and sunk into disturbed and half-conscious slumber. She was roused by a noise—and starting up to meet Leoni, saw a stranger in the act of putting aside the curtains of the window through which he was entering. Excess of terror made her speechless for a moment; when the man, who was in the garb of a boatman said,

"For the love of the saints, be calm, lady! I would lay down my life in your service; just hear me."

Lolah now recognised Stefano, who had before their marriage brought her many a note and flower from Leoni.

"Is the Count within?" asked he anxiously.

"I expect him every instant; but tell me your business at this strange hour."

Stefano hesitated.

"Perhaps it were best I should, and yet—do you know where I could find his Excellency?"
Lolah shook her head mournfully.

"Lady, I must then tell you all;" and he looked aside, and spoke hastily, as if unwilling to watch the misery his words must cause. "Lady, to-morrow this palace will be seized by the officers of the Inquisition, the Count—now St. Rosalie punish his enemies!—is accused of sorcery—to-morrow he will be arrested. My brother is one of their servants; but the Count is our old patron—he gave me a hint—I rowed hither—by means of a fishing-hook I fastened a rope to the balcony, and sprung up: I know every room of the palace, and thought to take my chance of meeting the Count Leoni; my boat lies below—a ship will sail from the bay at the break of day—they need sail fast, for they have better wine aboard than they would wish to have known in Palermo."

"Holy Virgin! if my husband should not return!" exclaimed Lolah, wringing her hands in agony. Stefano had not a word of comfort for such an emergency. Suddenly the Countess rose from her seat: "I will trust in the blessed saints for his return: what is the latest period that we can escape?"

"It will not be light this half hour, and I will answer for his safe pilotage while dark; but if the day once break, the fishermen will be abroad, and there will not be a chance of escape."

Lolah sank on her knees, and remained for a few moments with her face hidden between her hands in earnest prayer. Rising from the ground, she hastily addressed Stefano.

"Will you remain here and wait as long as you dare for the Count's arrival? I will return in a few minutes; I only go to make some brief preparation for our flight."

"Your flight?" ejaculated the boatman, "you are in no danger."

"It matters not," answered she passionately; "I will not leave my husband's side."

Ten minutes had scarcely elapsed, when she reappeared in a plain dark travelling dress, and dragging with her a large horseman's cloak.

"This will conceal him, as he must stay for no change of apparel. But can it be so long? why, it is a quarter of an hour since you told me we had but half a one?" and the gay and fairy chime of the timepiece told four o'clock.

"It is very dark still," said she, looking from the window.

"Yes, lady, it is very dark, the moon set an hour ago; but do not you lean out, the night-dew is falling heavily."

Again Lolah turned to the timepiece, the hand marked that five minutes more had passed away; she looked to Stefano, but he only shook his head and muttered some indistinct sound. A little rosary of coral and of the many-coloured lavas of Vesuvius hung at her waist—she prized it, for it was her dead mother's gift to her in her earliest childhood, and it was linked with the hope and affection of other years: her hand trembled so that she could not count the beads, but she repeated the prayers, at first audibly, and then the words died away in faint murmurs; at length she herself knew not what she was uttering. Her cheek, which had been pale as the funereal marble, burned with crimson, her lips were white and apart—the fever of her mind had communicated itself to her frame. With an unsteady step she again approached the balcony—"Tell me," said she, faintly, "is there a grey streak amid those clouds? I cannot see."

"Lady, it is still dark; hist!" at this moment, a distant step was heard in the corridor; nothing but hearing, made intense by anxiety, could have caught it.

"Mother of God! I thank thee, it is Leoni!"

She sprang forward; but her head grew dizzy, and she leant for a moment against the table for support. Leoni entered the room, haggard with his excited vigil, his cloak disordered, his rich vest open at the throat, as if in the agitation of the gaming-table he had loosened it to give himself air; a contraction, seemingly habitual, darkened his forehead; he was young still, but the expression and colours of youth were gone. He advanced moodily and abstractedly, when his eye was caught by the appearance of Stefano, who had lost not a moment in fastening the coils of the rope to the balcony.

"Robber!" shouted he; but the hand which sought his sword was arrested by Lolah's light touch on his arm.

"Be still, for your sweet life's sake," said she, in an earnest whisper, that fixed his attention at once; "yonder faithful creature has risked his for your's; we must fly, or to-morrow dawns for you in the dungeons of the Inquisition; all is ready for flight, only come."

Leoni turned still paler; then rallying with the high courage of his race, exclaimed, "Who dares accuse me? and what is my crime?"

"That matters not," said Stefano; "My brother gave me the hint; you fly to-night or are a prisoner in the morning. In the name of the good St. Rosalie, don't stand talking; you have lost time enough already; we have settled everything while waiting for you;—as if any good Christian ever kept such hours!" but these last words were muttered in an undertone.

"Come, my husband, there will be opportunity enough for explanation; fling this cloak round you, and follow me," said the Countess, stepping onwards.

"Never, Lolah," rejoined Montefiore, startled by the danger, which a conscious feeling in his own heart foreboded was true; "never shall you be exposed to the hardship and danger of such a flight, for me, so worthless, so neglectful!" But she was already at the foot of the ladder.

"Come, Signor; ten minutes more, and we are lost!"

Leoni followed, though almost unconsciously; and in an instant more, Stefano was steering his boat into the bay.

"Lolah, why are you here?" burst from him in the bitter accents of self-reproach, as he felt her head sink on his shoulder.

"Nay, my Leoni," said the low sweet voice on which he once hung with such passionate love, "where should I be but where rests all my earthly happiness? with my head on your heart, Leoni, love mine, I am very, very happy!"

Gently his arm enfolded the confiding and childlike form that rested upon him, and all the memory of their early tenderness gushed into his thoughts; while she, with a woman's engrossing devotedness, forgot everything but that her husband was once more her own.

"You must just pass for two runaways," said Stefano, "who have bribed me to row you beyond a powerful noble's reach, and who mean to stay from Palermo, till, for the daughter's sake, the lover is forgiven."

"Whither are we going?" asked Montefiore.

"On board yonder vessel, which bears a smuggling cargo; and pray you, at the port where she stops, lose no time in embarking for another. Do you remember the Marchese di Gonzarga?"

"Ay, the stripling! the sweeping away of whose ducats is the only instance of luck that ever awaited me at that accursed rouge-et-noir table."

"I doubt you owe something of your present plight to him; he is nephew to the Grand Inquisitor."

"And my husband is then the victim of his vile revenge!" cries the Countess, in a tone of delight.

Stefano made no answer: the next moment they were close to the ship, and he, fastening the boat to its side by a rope, sprung on board, to be spokesman for the party. Lolah trembled as the fragile bark rocked to and fro beneath the dark stern of the vessel, from which hung a lantern, whose dim light showed what she deemed their perilous position. Leoni might have felt the beating of the heart pillowed on his own; but he had himself been so long the sole object of his thoughts, that his wife's fear, not being shared by himself, never entered his mind.

"How provoking it is that I should have lost my last rouleau! I have not a ducat; and you hurried me so, that I had no time to bring away anything!" exclaimed he, peevishly. "What the devil terms shall we come to with these rascals, without money?"

"I have here three rouleaux," said the Countess; "I should have brought away more gold, but for its weight—I therefore preferred my diamonds, as to their sale we must look for our future support."

A smile passed over Montefiore's face; dearly did Lolah love his smile; but now rather, a thousand times rather would she have met his darkest frown.

"All is settled; you are to give the Captain fifty crowns on arriving in port; for the sake of his own pretty Agata, he said he would not be hard upon two young lovers:—I thought," added Stefano, in a whisper, "I might so promise, as I knew my lady had brought jewels away with her."

"Give me the rouleaux," said the Count, "and do you take them, Stefano; and when I return I will increase them a hundredfold."

"Keep your money, good your Excellency; what I have done was in honour and love for your noble house. Keep your gold; it would little benefit me, I trow!"

Leoni rose in anger, and began hastily to ascend the side of the ship. Stefano helped the Countess, who, as with his aid she climbed the knotted ropes, whispered,

"Take the gold, and lay it out in masses at the shrine of St. Rosalie, and this ring—my father gave it me; he will thankfully redeem it, and bless you, as his child does now."

"Come, come, Stefano, here's what will furnish you with many a merry night;" and Montefiore again pressed the money into Stefano's hand, who did not now reject it: the voice in which he muttered his good wishes was inaudible; and as he sprang into his boat, the tears of a three-year-old child stood in the eyes of the hardy rower. The Captain civilly showed the fugitives into a small cabin; and a fresh breeze, filling the sails, bore them rapidly from Sicily.

Next morning, all was astonishment and consternation in Palermo; there was the palace with its splendid ornaments, its almost regal train of servants; there were the gorgeous dresses, there were the golden caskets filled with jewels and perfumes; but where were the Count and Countess? The domestics searched every room in dismay; not only were they gone, but not a vestige remained of their flight. A strange suspicion rose in every mind, pale and affrighted they crowded together, and then surmise found speech. What if the demon, for whose wealth their lord had bartered his immortal soul—what if he had exacted, at length, his fearful tribute: had he carried off his victim bodily? But then the Countess, their gentle and pious mistress, could she be involved in such awful doom?—A loud knocking at the portal broke off their discourse; every one hurried to the door—to admit the officers of the Inquisition. All search was fruitless, all inquiry vain. The palace was confiscated, and its rich furniture sold; the Marchese di Montefiore was summoned to appear on a charge of sorcery; he came not to answer the accusation, and sentence of outlawry was passed against him. A thousand wild rumours were afloat, which finally merged in one—that unearthly retribution had been exacted for unearthly riches. Yet there were two in Palermo who knew the truth; the father of Lolah who died shortly after, a lonely and broken-hearted man; and Stefano—but he kept the secret as one of life and death; and when he perished in a storm at sea, it was buried with him in the deep and fathomless waters.

But now to return to our fugitives. At the first port they touched, they re-embarked, and finally landed at Marseilles; a small but lovely cottage on the seashore received them, an olive plantation encircled the house, and the Provence rose looked in at the casements. The far plains were covered with heath and thyme on one side, and on the other was the sea, where the rich vessels of the merchants seemed to sail to and fro forever. Fear and fatigue had severely tried a frame so frail as that of Lolah; and her husband's apprehension on her account for a time recalled his love:—perhaps they are more inseparable than we are ready to admit. Leoni felt that he was the only link between Lolah and life—his care the barrier between her and death: at length his gentle watchfulness was rewarded by the smile returning to her lip, and the rose to her cheek. Lolah thought she was very happy; in truth, from her birth, nature and fortune had been at variance: her delicate health unfitted her for either crowds or late hours—a constitutional timidity made her shrink from strangers—she had neither the talents which require, nor the spirits which enjoy an enlarged sphere of action: the affectionate monotony of her present life was just suited to her.

Not so to her husband, who soon desired more activity, more variety, more excitement: a thousand times did he ask himself of what avail was his boundless wealth, if he made it not the minister of pleasure? Every evening that he marked the sea redden beneath the setting sun, he vowed it should be the last. At length he resolved on leaving their cottage; and, after travelling for a few days, they settled in a superb château near Lyons. Lolah trembled at the magnificence which again surrounded them. Once she ventured to remonstrate on their lavish expenditure; but Leoni only laughed, and said, "You will not find here the miserable superstition of the Sicilians; and great part of my wealth was placed abroad. First we will dazzle these provincials, and then proceed to Paris."

In fact, Leoni feared yet to enter that most caravanserai-like capital; he wished to be somewhat forgotten of his countrymen, before he risked meeting with them. Half Lyons was soon collected at the château; what was splendour to Leoni, unless it were envied and admired? Perhaps the secret of his character was, that he was a very vain man, and yet had nothing in himself whereby that vanity was gratified; this forced him upon external resources. Again he delighted in bewildering by his magnificence, and astonishing by its extent. But in this enjoyment Lolah took no part; in this new display of riches, she saw but a confirmation of the suspicions which had driven them from Palermo: and Leoni—to whom, in spite of his selfishness, her devotion, her uncomplaining abandonment of home, friends, name, for his sake, had endeared her more and more, and who felt that Lolah was his only link with the past, the sole remembrance of his early and happy youth—Leoni felt bitterly the barrier that doubt drew between his wife and himself. He was mortified to think that his very power degraded him in her eyes; that she confounded him with the alchymists and sorcerers, whom he despised as they were despised in that military and feudal age. A thousand times he was on the point of revealing his secret, and then again the memory of the secrecy so mysteriously enjoined arose within him. A visitor at their fêtes, a passer-by on the road, who caught sight of the youthful couple, would have envied their happiness; but whosoever could have looked within on the hidden depths of their troubled minds, would have seen fear, discontent, sorrow for the past, and misgiving for the future.

One night there was a superb entertainment; the Countess presided, pale and melancholy; the Count, weary of himself, and therefore of his guests, secretly compared them with the brilliant groups that had assembled in his palazzo at Palermo, and thought how little his provincial set were worthy of the cost and taste bestowed upon them. In reality, display had lost its novelty, and consequently its charm in his eyes. The evening had not half passed away, when Lolah was astonished by his coming up to her and whispering, "For Heaven's sake, find some excuse for dismissing these people! Illness will do; for I am sure you look pale enough."

She might have re-echoed her husband's words, for he himself looked wild and haggard. Still, it was near midnight when their guests dispersed; and Leoni—on returning from conducting la Presidente de Lanville, always the latest of the late, to her huge family coach—silently approached one of the windows, and stepping out upon the terrace, stood as if absorbed in the lovely view—and lovely indeed it was. Below, was a smooth turf, which sloped down to a lake, whose surface reflected the moonshine broken and tremulous; the moon herself was rising on the other side of the château, and so was invisible; but her light lay silvery on the grass, and lent a softness, sweeter even than colour, to many-shaped beds, which were filled with flowers. In the middle of the garden was a fountain; to a certain height the water shot up in a bright and straight column, suddenly the stream divided and came down in a glittering shower to the marble basin below, and the falling of this fountain was the only sound that broke the perfect stillness. A quiet step approached, a soft hand was laid on his arm, and Lolah whispered, "Is it not beautiful?" How often will the lip frame some indifferent question, when the heart is full of the most important!

"Will you then regret to leave it?" said Leoni, as they wandered throughout the maze of odoriferous flower-pots, "for we must go to-morrow."

Lolah gazed upon his face, but words died on her lips.

"That wearisome Madame de Lanville," continued he, "entertained me this evening with her delight that she should soon have a worthy guest to introduce to me; for that in a week's time the Count Gonzaga, the nephew of the great cardinal, would spend a few days at her house, on his way to the south of France; and she was so sure I should find him a charming acquaintance. Plague on the old simpleton, and the Count too! what cursed chance brings him here?"

"My Leoni, why should you fear him!" murmured Lolah.

"Fear him, nonsense! But it would be very disagreeable to have the old and foolish story which banished us from Palermo, set abroad in Lyons:" and, lost in gloomy meditation, he sank on a carved stone seat by the lake. For a moment the Countess stood irresolute by his side—suddenly dropping on one knee, she leant her beautiful head on his arm, and watching his countenance with those eloquent eyes which had never looked upon him but in love, said, in a low pleading voice,

"Leoni, mine, my heart has never had one thought hidden from you, how can you bear to shut yours so utterly from me?"

He made her no answer except by kissing her eyes, as if he might not see and resist their eloquent pleading: but his young wife had gained courage—the worst was over—and her very fondness, which made his anger such a thing of fear, now urged her to endeavour to persuade, if she could not convince. She implored him to say what was the secret of his wealth; to justify its possession if possible—if not, to fling it from him: what lot could there be in life which she would not be ready to share with him? Had his wealth made him happy? oh, no! it had sown division between them; it had exiled him from his own land; it was now about to force him to become a wanderer again.

"I tell you, my beloved husband, this secret is to me even as death; I kneel to the Madonna, and my thoughts are not with prayer; in society I shrink from every eye with a vague but ever-present fear—a word, a look, sends the colour from my cheek, and curdles the life-blood at my heart; and yet I know not what I dread: and sleep, oh, sleep is very terrible! for then, Leoni, you tell me what it is death to hear, and I start from my pillow—but when I waken I disbelieve your guilt:—you guilty, Leoni? oh, no! no!" and again her head sank, while the moonlight fell on her pale cheek, and eyes glistening with earnestness and tears.

Weak and self-indulgent, accustomed to yield in all things to the impulse of the moment, Leoni was a very unfit person to be intrusted with a mystery and a secret: he sufficed not to himself; he felt weary of his unshared thoughts; and at this moment he was irresolute—he would even have wished to throw all the responsibility of decision on the fragile and gentle creature by his side.

In the deep stillness of that moonlit midnight he told her all; his voice died in silence, which was interrupted by a faint shriek from his wife; she pointed to the lake, but strong terror made her speechless—a faint silvery outline of a form was seen in the distant air; it came nearer, and the shadow fell dark upon the wave; a stately and lovely female slowly advanced across the water, which yielded not beneath her shining feet. The flashing of her radiant eyes fell upon the culprit—she raised her hand, whereon shone the starry talisman as it shone when she bade the spirits give him wealth unbounded and at a wish. She beckoned Leoni. A power was on him which forced him to obey—he sprang towards the lake—he sank below the surface—twice he emerged from the bright waves, again they closed over his head, and the moon shone upon one unbroken line of light. The strange and beautiful being gazed on the spot with a look of horror; she wrung her hands as if in the helplessness of despair—a low cry came upon the wind, and its mysterious utterer had disappeared. An influence stronger than even fear or love had riveted Lolah like a statue to the place; but as that figure melted into air, a terrible life returned to her—she rushed towards the lake, and with one wild shriek plunged into its depths.

Next morning, the birds were singing among the boughs, the bees were gathering their early honey amid the flowers, the sun had turned the lake into a sheet of gold—when the servants were drawn to the spot by a light-blue scarf floating on the waters; they knew it was what their mistress had worn the night before. The silver flowers embroidered on it, glittering in the sunshine, first caught the eye; assistance was procured, and the bodies were soon found. The wreath of white lilies yet bound the raven tresses of Lolah, some of whose lengths had become entangled round the neck of her husband. They parted them not, but carried them to the château. Ere noon, every inhabitant of Lyons had mourned over their youthful, but marble-like beauty. None knew their history; none ever solved the mystery of their fate—but there were many affectionate hearts that grew sorrowful for their sake—and kind hands buried them together in the same grave.

One morning a marble urn was found upon their tomb, though none could tell who placed it there. On it was exquisitely carved a veiled female figure, with hands clasped as if in prayer, and head bowed down as if weeping; she was kneeling at the foot of the Cross: a scroll below was graven with one single

THE TALISMAN

"The other side—the other side is where foot-passengers pay."

Charles mechanically obeyed the direction.

"One penny, sir!"

He was roused at once from his abstraction; for it was a question to himself whether he had even that in his pocket. Sixpence was, however, discovered; he paid the toll, and passed on. But the impetus of his resolution was gone: out on the certainty of human resolve! Charles had meditated weeks on the act he was about to commit; his reasonings had brought conviction both of the necessity and of the right of suicide; he stood ruined in fortune, desperate, and, as he believed, determined; yet the fact of having had to pay a penny on his road to destruction made him pause. He stayed to recover the excitement of his imagination in one of the recesses of the bridge; involuntarily, as he leaned over the balustrade, his eye became attracted by surrounding objects: he was startled to perceive how light it was. "Pleasant," thought he, "when the fearful plunge has been taken, and the last struggle is over, to find yourself roused from that stupor which had been even as death, by bottles of hot water at your feet, a stomach-pump in your mouth, an old woman rubbing you down with flannel, and a respectable member of the Humane Society watching the first moment of returning consciousness, in order to point out the horror of your crime! No, no; not now, with witnesses and succour at hand; but in the dark night, when the stars alone behold what their shining records may long since have prophesied, then shall the waters, gloomy as the life they close, give me that repose—death."

Content with this determination, he gladly allowed his attention to fix on the scene before him. Nowhere are the many contrasts in the appearance of our metropolis more strikingly assembled than in the view from Waterloo Bridge. As yet the sunshine, which produces the deep shadows deeper for its own brightness, was only prophesied by the clear gray light that brought out every object in the same dim but distinct atmosphere. The large pale lamps were not yet extinguished; but they gave no light, save to the dark arches of Somerset House, whose depths they seemed vainly striving to penetrate.

Somerset House conveys the idea of a Venetian palace; its Corinthian pillars, its walls rising from the waters, its deep arches, fitting harbours for the black gondola, the lion sculptured in the carved arms— all realises the picture which the mind has of those marble homes where the Foscarini and the Donati dwelt, in those days when Venice was at her height of mystery and magnificence. The other side is, on the contrary, just the image of a Dutch town; the masses of floating planks, the low tile-covered buildings, the crowded warehouses—mean, dingy, but full of wealth and industry—are the exact semblance of the towns which, like those of the haughty bride of the Adriatic, rose from the very bosom of the deep—Amsterdam and Venice. The history of the Italians is picturesque and chivalric; but that of the Dutch has always seemed to me the beau-ideal of honourable industry, rational exertion, generally enjoyed liberty, and all strong in more than one brave defence. He does not deserve to read history, who does not enjoy the gallant manner in which they beat back Louis XIV.

"The two banks of the river embody the English nation," thought Charles; "there is its magnificence and its poetry, its terraces, its pillars, and its carved emblazonings; and on the other is its trade, its industry, its warehouses, and their many signs of skill and toil. Ah! the sun is rising over them, as if in encouragement: I here take the last lesson of my destiny. I have chosen the wrong side of the river— forced upon exertion, what had I to do with the poetry of life?"

The river became at every instant more beautiful; long lines of crimson light trembled in the stream; fifty pointed spires glittered in the bright air, each marking one of those sacred fanes where the dead find a hallowed rest, and the living a hallowed hope. In the midst arose the giant dome of St. Paul's—a mighty shrine, fit for the thanksgiving of a mighty people. As yet, the many houses around lay in unbroken repose; the gardens of the Temple looked green and quiet, as if far away in some lonely valley; and the few solitary trees scattered among the houses seemed to drink the fresh morning air and rejoice.

"How strong is the love of the country in all indwellers of towns!" exclaimed Charles. "How many creepers, shutting out the dark wall, can I see from this spot! how many pots of bright-coloured and sweet-scented plants are carefully nursed in windows, which, but for them, would be dreary indeed! And yet even here is that wretched inequality in which fate delights alike in the animate and inanimate world. What have those miserable trees and shrubs done, that they should thus be surrounded by an unnatural world of brick—the air, which is their life, close and poisoned, and the very rain, which should refresh them, but washing down the soot and dust from the roofs above; and all this, when so many of their race flourish in the glad and open fields, their free branches spreading to the morning dews and the summer showers, while the earliest growth of violets springs beneath their shade?" He turned discontentedly to the other side of the bridge.

"Beautiful!" was his involuntary ejaculation.

The waves were freighted as if with Tyrian purple, so rich was the sky which they mirrored; the graceful arches of Westminster Bridge stretched lightly across, and, shining like alabaster, rose the carved walls of the fine old Abbey, where sleep the noblest of England's dead. Honour to the glorious past!—how it honoured us! Once we were the future, and how much was done for our sake!—The contrast between above and below the bridge is very striking. Below, all seems for use, except Somerset House—and even that, when we think, is but a superb office—and the Temple gardens: all is crowded, dingy, and commercial. Above, wealth has arrived at luxury; and the grounds behind Whitehall, the large and ornamental houses, have all the outward signs of rank and riches.

Charles turned sullenly from them, and watched the boats now floating with the tide. As yet few were in motion; the huge barges rested by the banks, but two or three colliers came on with their large black sails, and darkened the glistening river as they passed. At this moment, the sweet chimes of St. Bride struck five, and the sound was immediately repeated by the many clocks on every side: for an instant the air was filled with music.

"Curious it is," murmured our hero, "that every hour of our day is repeated from myriad chimes; and yet how rarely do we attend to the clock striking! Alas! how emblematic is this of the way in which we neglect the many signs of time! How terrible, when we think of what time may achieve, is the manner in which we waste it! At the end of every man's life, at least three-quarters of the mighty element of which that life was composed will be found void—lost—nay, utterly forgotten! And yet that time, laboured and husbanded, might have built palaces, gathered wealth, and, still greater, made an imperishable name."

He was awakened from a long but common meditation on what he might have done, and what he had not done, by a grumbling voice.

"How dirty the Thames is! they say the gas kills every fish in the river; yet I suppose it is thought good enough for Christians. Well, well, everything changes for the worse; I am sure the water was clear enough in my young days. But we shall never get on, if we stay chattering here: do make haste, child!"

So saying, an old woman hurried on, bending beneath a heavy basket; and at her side ran one of those wan, under-sized children, ragged, dirty, and meagre, among the most sorrowful spectacles of sorrowful humanity. Poverty is a terrible thing when it bows to the very ground the pride of the strong man—a terrible thing when it leaves old age destitute: still, the strong man may yet redeem his fortunes, and that old age may have had enjoyment while it was capable of enjoying. But a child, with the step slow from weakness, which from its age should be so buoyant; a cheek thin and white from hunger, at a period which especially cares for food (for all children are greedy); a form shrivelled with cold; a growth stopped by work too laborious for such tender years; a spirit broken by toil, want, and harshness;—is not such a child poverty's most miserable spectacle? It is, however, a common one.

Off they went, the old woman and her grandson; she scolding the poor boy because the Thames was muddy; and he shrinking fearfully, lest anger might find blows more availing than words. Yet that aged creature's irritation was a sort of kindness: it was for his sake that she laboured out her last strength; and while the tones were shrill and cross, she was thinking how she could best procure food for the sickly child.

Charles's meditations were effectually disturbed; he left his seat in the recess, and hurried indignantly forward.

"And suffering like this!" thought he—"suffering that crushes alike youth and age, from which the innocence of childhood is not protected, and against which the experience of age cannot guard!—exists in our mighty, our magnificent city, whose very will is dominion on the earth. Look how she ministers to her pleasures!" Just then his eye fell upon the two enormous buildings, our national theatres.

"Look at those vast edifices, so vast where space is such an object! There, while weeping for sorrows which are not, laughing at the light jest or the ludicrous misadventure, how little is remembered of the want which makes fear the only bond that binds the living to life!"

This current of reproach was, however, interrupted by the recollection, that, after all, this very relaxation gave support to many; and that, in the case of the majority who enjoyed it, it had been fairly earned by toil, which, like the bow, needed to be unbent. His imagination, too, warmed with the thought of what glorious triumphs those roofs had witnessed—the passionate creation of the poet, the living personification of the actor: he remembered the eloquent words that stir the noblest fountains of our being, and decided on the general right to enjoy such generous pleasure.

"Good and evil! good and evil!" thought he; "ye are mingled inextricably in the web of our being; and who may unthread the darker yarn?"

He was here jostled at once from his reverie and his side of the pavement. He had wandered through many streets, and now found himself under one of the piazzas of Covent Garden: it was no place for an idle person; all were hurrying to and fro; all was employment and business. On he went into the market. How fresh, how sweet everything, and how industrious every body looked! There were the stalls of the vegetables, with their pure and wholesome smell of the freshly turned-up earth; others with fruit—the delicate crimson strawberries, each spotted with gold; the cherries, with their rich varieties of hues—the deep ruby, almost black or coral, as if the moisture of the wave yet lingered upon it—and amber, with one trickling stain of red, so fancifully denominated the "bleeding heart." Further on was a stall of foreign fruits: the pale cool lemon; the red gold of the orange; the pine—with its yellow carved globe, and its coronal of silvery green—the architectural pine, so rich and so massive. But most beautiful of all, shewing the deep delight the heart takes in loveliness, were the stands of many flowers. There they crowded in fragrant multitudes, each kind tied up in separate bunches; the yellow lupin, like "a clump of shining spears;" pinks, each with the dark central spot, like the purple and painted stain round the eye of an eastern sultana; the light branches of the small saffron flowers, of that deep blue so rare among "the painted populace," which seem to delight in gayer dyes; the sweet pea, with its wings of the butterfly, its colours of the rainbow; and roses, in all their infinite variety—the white, like driven snow; the soft pink, almost as lovely as the maiden's blush which gives it its name; the parti-coloured damask, the chivalric and historic rose, recalling the fierce combats of York and Lancaster; and the moss, so beautiful in the bud,—all lay heaped together, as if Summer had been conquered, and here were gathered its spoils.

While Charles loitered to and fro, he was forcibly reminded that he was in the way; every train of thought was broken in upon by some hurried passer-by; and yet how orderly, how quiet, was all this bustle! How many of the stalls hung out fragile glass globes, filled with gold and silver fish! But they were in the ordinary run of business—he was not. A long and dreary day was yet before him; how was it to be passed? If he returned to his lodgings, he must invent some plausible plea for his reappearance, after having taken his farewell as for a long journey. Impossible! his spirits were too heavy for invention. Spend the day at a coffee-house? he had now only five pence in the world. Call on some friend, and be expected to sympathise in their sorrow, or share in their mirth, while his own thoughts were numbering the hours, each of which brought him nearer to the grave? No; he would wander about the city, and watch those processes of humanity in which he had no longer a share.

At that moment, a human want was uppermost in his mind—he was hungry. Seated on a little wooden stool, his boiler supported by a three-legged trivet, over a small pan of burning charcoal, on one side, and a basket covered with a white cloth on the other, an old man was selling rolls and coffee to the market-people. The fresh air of the morning had had the same effect upon Charles as on the peasantry. The old man never looked at his customer; prince or ploughman it was all the same to him, so that he sold his rolls and coffee. Charles had finished his breakfast before he recollected what folly it was to sustain that life which was so soon to terminate. A single penny remained of his sixpence; he gave it to a beggar at hand, as much from thoughtlessness as from charity, and yet the woman bade God bless him!

Life was now fully astir in the city, morning—which is so beautiful in the country, with its long shadows, its lucid sunshine, and its glittering dew—in town is the meanest part of the day, seemingly devoted to cleanliness and hunger. Carpets are being shaken from the windows, the steps are being washed, and the butcher with his tray, the baker with his basket, the grocer, and the milkman, hurry from door to door; and day, like life, has first its necessaries, and then its luxuries. Charles wandered on among the hurrying throng, referring them only to himself.

"How little," thought he, "do these people—thus busy in the many preparations of existence how little do they deem, that among them walks one who is with them, not of them; one consecrated by death!"

Strange that this idea carried with it something of exultation! so much does the pride of man rejoice in aught that marks him from his fellows, and little does it seem to matter whether that mark be for good or for evil. There must be some deep-rooted anti-social principle in every man's nature, so dearly does he love aught that separates him from his kind; or is it but one of the many shapes taken by that mental kaleidoscope, vanity, the varying and the glittering, the desire of distinction, sinking into that of notice? Charles's was just an exciting consciousness; and he paced the streets, sometimes roused into disdain of the busy and thoughtless crowd around, but oftener lost in gloomy dreams of that futurity whose depths he was so soon to explore. Suddenly the air was filled with fragrance, which came from a balcony where the heliotrope was growing in great luxuriance. He started at its well-known perfume; he stood by the very door he had sworn never to re-enter—by the dwelling of the cold, the beautiful Laura Herbert.

What an atmosphere of luxury was around the house! The balustrades of the balcony were of white, and carved, whose vacant spaces were filled with the rarest exotics; an entablature of antique figures ran below the roof. Could the ancient temple they first adorned have shrined a fairer divinity? He saw the amber silk curtains wave to and fro: the middle window was open; in it stood a pillar of lapis lazuli, which supported an alabaster figure, Canova's Dansatrice. And there she dwelt, who might have given him wealth, love, and life; but who left him to penury, despair, and death. She—for whose sake he had abandoned all the pursuits that once made his hope and his happiness; who had turned his course of contented study into a delirious fever; who was the cause that he now stood on the threshold of the grave—why should she have freedom and wealth, while he was consumed by passion, and weighed down by poverty?

A carriage drove up to the door; well he knew the crimson window-blinds, which had so often shed their rich colour on her cheek. Charles rushed away; he could not have borne to see that fairy foot descend the steps, or have met, though only for a moment, those bewildering eyes. But the thread of his reverie was broken; the image of death no longer filled his mind. He thought of life, its enjoyments, its desires, all from which he was cut off in his youth: he thought of the poor, and he loathed them; of the rich, and he hated them.

"Accursed destiny!" he muttered; "so young, so capable of happiness, and yet without the means! Why have I talents to which I can never do justice? Why have I tastes I can never gratify? Why do I want for that luxury my penury denies? Why am I refined in my habits? Why have I thoughts and feelings entirely at variance with my condition? Why have not my birth, my education, and my estate gone together, instead of being so utterly opposed? Why at this moment am I friendless, penniless, and hopeless? Alas! with the delight I have lost the power of exertion. Well, Death finishes this weary struggle. Death! mighty, glorious, and triumphant Death! if thou hadst not existed before, I must have invented thee as a resource."

But in vain Charles sought to regain his gloomy tranquillity. He then endeavoured to fix his attention on outward objects; they could only give food to his discontent: the splendid equipages hurrying past, the glittering shops, the gay crowd now beginning to appear, brought with them the images of ungratified wishes and painful contrasts. He turned into a by street, where a stall of old books caught his eye; mechanically he opened them one after another, till at last his attention became riveted on an almost worn-out volume of ancient ballads. Of itself, it opened at Chevy Chase—

"The stout Earl of Northumberland
    A vow to God did make.
His pleasure in the Scottish woods
    Three summer days to take."

"How perfectly," thought he, "does this set forth the whole spirit of the age—its love of war and of the chase, and its superstition! The feudal chieftain is not content with the chase unless it be in an enemy's ground, and actually believes in his own mind that he hallows this act of aggression by calling God to witness his resolve. How characteristic is the meeting between the two earls, and the interference of the squire, who protests against their followers standing by as mere pacific spectators!

'I would not have it told
    To Henry, our king, for shame.'

A brief dialogue between the two combatants embodies the whole spirit of chivalry:

'Yield thee, Lord Percy, Douglas said—
Thy ransom I will freely give.
    And thus report of thee—

Thou art the most courageous knight
     That ever I did see.

No, Douglas, quoth Earl Percy then,
     Thy proffer I do scorne;
I will not yeilde to any Scot
     That ever yet was borne.'

Again, when Earl Douglas has received 'his deepe and deadlye blow,' death is nothing compared with his bitter consciousness that 'Earl Percy sees me fall.' Homer, they say, always favoured the Grecians, as being his countrymen. The heroic minstrel of Chevy Chase is equally national; for when the tidings of Earl Douglas's death arrive in Scotland—

'O heavy news! King James did say;
     Scotland can witnes bee,
I have not any captaine more
     Of such account as hee.'

In London, the case is quite different:
'Now, God be with him! said our king,
     Sith 'twill not better bee;
I trust I have within my realm
     Five hundred good as hee.'"

Suddenly he flung the book down, and walked hurriedly away. "What folly," he inwardly exclaimed, "is that hope which is at once the cause and the reward of poetry! The author of this brief epic has done all that poet could do: he has given immortality to all that was held precious in his time; its chivalric daring, its true faith, its loyalty; he has duly exalted the supremacy of his native land,—and yet he is forgotten! The song remains, but the memory of the singer has passed away. Who pauses to think in what poverty, in what obscurity, in what wretchedness, the writer of that noble ballad may have wasted a desolate and a disappointed existence? Did he die young, poisoned by the first draught of life and its sorrows? or did he drag on a weary old age, whose hope had long since perished? Who knows? and, alas! who cares? We take our pleasure, and we think not of gratitude. Out upon the accursed and selfish race to which I belong! Even so have I laboured, and even so shall I be rewarded. Fool that I have been! to toil hour after hour in giving others—what?—an hour's gratification, which they will take thanklessly, and even reproachfully, full of their own petty cavillings and distastes. The peasant boy, who followed the coloured track of the rainbow, hoping to find the blue and charmed flower which springs where the arch touches earth, is wiser far than one who gives youth, genius, and time to literature. Half the exertion, and a tithe of the talent, would, if directed to another pursuit, win for him, if not 'golden opinions,' yet gold in reality; and what can make life endurable in this world but wealth?"

In the next street the doors of an auction-room stood open, where the articles were on view previous to the morrow's sale; there he resolved to seek amusement. As he entered the clock struck two.

"It will be lonely and dark on the Thames by ten; so I have just eight hours more to live."

The room was filled with all that ingenuity could invent, or luxury wish—all that taste could select, or wealth purchase. The spoils of a palace built and furnished by the most magnificent of misanthropes—

the collection of a life—were being dispersed in the caprice of a day. There was the alabaster vase, carved in snow, to which some spell had given stability; small precious cups of onyx and agate, such as might have stood at the right hand of the King and Queen of the Fairies when they had bidden their court to a moonlight banquet. Near was a table of maple-wood, veined like a wrist, but smooth and coloured as pale yellow satin. On it lay an Indian rosary of strung pearls; the fingers of the lovely Brahmin to whom it had once belonged, had left their fragrance on the string. There was a silver salver, over whose shining surface Cellini's delicate graver had scattered Spring: spiritual indeed were the small and graceful figures, whose minute outlines were yet perfect in their proportions; while the wreathe of flowers that encircled them seemed too fine to be the work of mortal hand. On the other side was placed a round table of Sevre china; a large medallion, representing the head of an angel—and an angel it surely was, if there be aught angelic in beauty—so pure, so placid was that lovely head! On it was set a basket of silver filigree, delicate as the threads of the morning gossamer: it must have been a skilful workman that wrought those fragile threads into their present intricate grace. Near it stood two small bronze figures of Voltaire and Rousseau. There was something singularly characteristic in the manner in which these philosophers grasped their canes: he of Ferney held his lightly, as if a touch could brush away any impediment from his path; but he of Geneva had his grasped with might and main, and driven into the earth, as if prepared to crush all that might rouse his fierce indignation. What a mistake rage is! anger should never go beyond a sneer, if it really desires revenge.

But a picture by Murillo fixed Charles's attention—one of those boys whose embrowned cheek glows with health, and whose dark eyes are filled with happiness—one of those pictures in which the Spanish artist concentrates so much of life's earlier existence—calling back that glad and buoyant frankness, whose loss is experience's first lesson. Near it hung a landscape by Salvator Rosa; a sky, every cloud of which was heavy with thunder; a lake, the troubled mirror of a troubled heaven; bleak rocks, that seemed to reverse the law of nature, and say, "Here life comes not—life which, in an animal or vegetable shape, teems on all other parts of the globe; but to us clings not one blade of grass;" and black woods, where the wild beast had its lair, or wilder man, who, casting off all social ties, lived but to war upon his kind. Close beside was a lovely valley by Claude Lorraine. From this Charles turned away: what sympathy had he with sunshine?—The genius of Salvator and of Byron alike asked immortality of pain. To the majority of mankind misery is a familiar thing: the dark colour and the mournful word find a home and an echo in every human heart.—Beneath stood a table made of mosaic from Pompeii. How many would admire the intricate blending of its varied colours, without giving a thought to the scene of mortal destruction and desolation from which it came! On it was a model in ivory of that most perfect specimen of Hindoo architecture, the stately temple which Jehanghire built as a tomb for his loved sultana the mighty dome, the many minarets, the hundred steps, the lofty walls, were all exquisitely wrought in miniature.

"I like," said Charles, "this monumental magnificence; it is a superb mockery. The marble is brought from a distant quarry; hundreds of slaves are employed to cut and polish it; and human talent taxes its invention to give it graceful proportion. The dome towers in the blue air, the noble columns rise above the funereal cypresses around; and for what?—to keep a handful of dust from being scattered by the winds, and to preserve a memory for which no one living cares."

A thousand splendid trifles lay glittering on a large table near:—flasks of crystal, redolent of eastern perfumes, some of which, spotted with gold, enclosed a whole summer of roses from Damietta—toys wrought in mother-of-pearl and amber, heaped up with the profusion of a mistress of some geni, who knows that the sylphs of the air and the gnomes of the mines toil to work her pleasure. Placed on a richly chased gold stand was a déjeûner of Sevre china, the cups painted with medallions of the beauties of Louis the Fourteenth's reign. Charles took up the one that bore the likeness of the lovely and ill-fated La Valliere.

"And is it possible," he asked, "that a face like this, so sweet and so touching, could ever become a familiar, even a tiresome thing—that a cup so precious as this could ever be put to the common uses of the table? There is a strange similarity in the fate of the china and of the face wrought in its colours. Both guarded for a time as favourite toys, grown weary of, neglected, and left to the many chances of destruction—till heart and cup are alike broken!" Close by stood a couch, covered with a spotted leopard's skin, and supported by claws of bronze. Charles threw himself upon it; how its luxurious softness mocked its material! The shadowy reveries of the dim future, to which he again yielded himself, were broken by some one speaking at his side:

"Perhaps, as you appear so much engaged in contemplation of our collection, you maybe disposed to become an immediate purchaser? I am authorised to treat by private contract."

"And who are you?" exclaimed Charles.

"The person employed to sell this property; very happy to treat with you, sir."

Assuredly there was nothing in the face of the auctioneer to induce confidence, particularly when that confidence related to the feelings. He was a spare, meagre man, who looked as if he saved even in himself; with the light hair and sallow skin which distinguish the Portuguese Jew especially, and the high nose and elevated eyebrow which mark the Jew all over the world:—a man who divided the human race into two classes, buyers and sellers; whose atmosphere was trade, the real of whose life was gain, and the ideal, wealth. Yet to this incarnation of the pence-table did Charles resolve to unfold his cause of loitering. Charles was vain and imaginative; vanity led him to be egotistical, and his imagination threw its grace over the confession, half of which it colours, if it does not create. He therefore stated to the auctioneer his desire of killing time, till he killed himself. At first the man looked aghast, then afraid, and at last suspicious that his visitor might intend to rob, nay, murder him. He drew back, and placed his hand upon the bell-rope; and having also ascertained that he was himself next the door, prepared to listen to the remainder with a keen suspicious look, which said, as plainly as look could, "You need not think to rob me; I'm up to a thing or two." Truth, however, carries its own conviction; and the auctioneer was under the necessity of believing that a person was before him who meditated destroying himself. Suddenly his features sharpened; something appeared to flash across his mind, or rather his memory.

"You are the very man!" said he, thinking aloud in his hurry.

A few words will explain this ejaculation.

Among the great riches and many curiosities which the gorgeous merchant had gathered, and now wished to disperse, was one that had been thus consigned to the agent:—"Sell it for any thing—nothing—give it away; only, get rid of it."

It was a square piece of shagreen, on which were inscribed some Hebrew characters.

"Sell it!" thought the auctioneer; "why, nobody would give him a farthing for it!"

Still, giving it away was against his principles; and principles, like facts, are stubborn things when founded on interest. One day, however, a Jew, with whom he had occasional dealings, threw a new light on the subject, by translating the inscription, which was as follows:

"In possessing me, you possess everything: but your life will be mine. Wish, and your wishes will be accomplished; but at every wish I shall diminish, as will your days. Regulate your wishes by your life, which will be in me. Wilt thou have me? Take me; and the Lord God have mercy upon you! Amen."

The shagreen skin was a talisman. The auctioneer felt exceedingly uncomfortable: the devil was the only individual with whom he desired to have no dealings. He was himself a man who, since his conversion, feared God and honoured the king, went to church on a Sunday, and never bought or sold stock on a Friday. All his transactions with the superb merchant, whose glittering spoils he was to bring to the hammer, had been quite out of the ordinary way of business. He had been summoned express from London: late in the evening he saw the moon rise over the shadowy turrets of the stately dwelling, whose interior was as much a mystery as its master. Before him stood the gigantic tower, built by torchlight; and of which it was said in the village, that in the course of a year all the workmen employed in its building had perished. The moaning of the wind in the gloomy branches was the only sound, save his horse's steps, in the yew-tree avenue which led to the house. He arrived: black slaves, silent as the grave, received him; and a white but hideous dwarf led him through the huge and lonely apartments, lighted by four mute flambeau-bearers. The signs of wealth scattered around so profusely, forced from him exclamations of surprise and admiration; but no reply was elicited, and no sound of human voice was heard in any of the sumptuous rooms through which he was conducted. Sign of food or firing there was none. At length they reached a chamber hung with tapestry: its half-faded colours made more ghastly the scene it represented—souls suffering in purgatory. The sheets of blue flame, the spectral figures which writhed in every attitude of pain, the wan and distorted faces, took a strange reality of horror from the high wind that shook the arras, and the flickering light flung over it by the waving torches.

In the midst of these pleasant objects of contemplation, at a little table, on which lay a large folio printed in unknown character, sat the master of the house—he who, it was said, shunned society, to dwell in unbroken and splendid solitude; whose light shone at midnight from the vast and lonely tower, but of whose pursuits all were ignorant. He was rather past the middle age, intellectual in face, and stately in figure; but the face was pale and care-worn, and the figure bent, as if from physical weakness. The loose black gown in which he was wrapped, gave him the appearance of an invalid, or of a recluse, to whom dress was matter of indifference.

"You have seen the baubles I destine for the fools who may fancy them; they shall all be sent to the city in the course of to-morrow: prepare your rooms for their reception, and attend to the sale."

The low, deep, sweet voice strongly contrasted with the fierce and abrupt manner; for the words were scarcely said, before, resting his head again upon his hands, he was immersed in his open volume. The dwarf motioned to the surprised auctioneer to leave the room, reconducted him through the costly but melancholy apartments, and left him to remount his horse in the yew-tree avenue, without offering either rest or refreshment, though the night was considerably advanced.

The bewildered auctioneer hurried on, divided by mingled fears of ghosts and thieves; the large and dismal branches of the yews, as they swung to and fro in the wind, causing him innumerable alarms. Every noise was taken for a robber, and every shadow for an apparition. However, he arrived in safety at the village inn, where as many marvels were related of the solitary owner of the mansion as mystery always creates. The whole secret was settled, by deciding that "he had something on his conscience;" and murder, that favourite sin of the vulgar, was fixed upon. What uncharitable things inferences and conclusions are! But the man who, whether in his habits or his actions, in great things or in small, separates himself from his kind, seems to set every evil and envious feeling of our nature in array against him. Distinction is purchased at the expense of sympathy.

The following day the treasures of the mysterious tower came pouring in: pictures, statues, gems, shells, china, stuffed beasts and birds, tables, vases, petrifactions, arms, mandarins, &c. &c.; and among them the shagreen skin, with the injunction, "Sell it for anything—nothing—give it away; only, get rid of it."

Who would buy it? or, indeed, who would take it, with the denunciation attached to its possession? The auctioneer became sincerely distressed; a cricket that had sung at his parlour-hearth for ten years suddenly departed; the black cat was missing; a strange dog howled at his steps for two successive nights; his wife had dreamt of gold and running water, the most unlucky things in the world; and then the times were so bad—the stocks were falling—the cholera coming—the sooner the shagreen skin was out of his house the better. Charles seemed, as he afterwards said, sent by Providence.

He forthwith mentioned the wonderful charm in his custody, dwelt upon its merits till he grew quite eloquent, and finally desired the youth to follow him to the inner room, where it hung. It was a small dark chamber, crowded with articles for sale; but, whether from accident or design, the curiosities were all of a wild and ghastly kind. In the middle was a cast of the Laocoon, the wretched father and his children writhing in the folds of the terrible serpents: cruel must have been the eye and heart of the sculptor who thus made agony his triumph. Against the wall leant an Egyptian mummy; part of the yellow linen had been unveiled, and a spectral likeness of humanity glared from between the bandages. Near it was one of the frightful idols of the Mexicans—a many-headed snake, whose crimson jaws seemed yet red with their human sacrifice: and in a corner stood some quivers of poisoned Indian arrows, and a gigantic battle-axe. To the left were terrific-looking engines, labelled as models of the instruments of torture found in the Inquisition.

Charles was allowed little time to gaze by the impatient auctioneer, who pointed at once to the shagreen skin, which lay on a black oak table. He read the inscription; and a strange feeling of vague belief, and desire for its possession, entered his heart. One wish for wealth, and then every enjoyment was at his feet; and truly, a few years of life were a slight sacrifice, considering that they would be taken from his old age. Not that he believed in any such nonsense—still, he should like to try. The auctioneer had been watching his eager look, as one accustomed to drive a hard bargain eyes his customer: his whole plan of action was arranged. A plum being his own ultimatum of fortune and felicity, he supposed that would also be the aim of his visitor: twenty per cent was in his opinion fair profit—he must not expect too much from such a mere speculation.

"You see, sir," turning to Charles, "desperate diseases require desperate remedies—you cannot be worse off, and you may be better. Sign this bond for twenty thousand pounds; if the skin answers, it is a bargain; if not, being, as you say, a beggar, the agreement is void—there can be no levy where there are no effects: and though I have heard of skinning a flint, I never yet could learn how it was managed."

Charles signed the bond, and seizing the shagreen skin, rushed away, exclaiming, "Now give me wealth—hundreds, thousands, millions!"

"Millions!" almost shrieked the auctioneer, aghast—"taken in, cheated, robbed—stop thief!" but his customer was lost in the darkness which had by this time set in. Again Charles wandered through the streets, with that indifference as to what direction which spoke the pre-occupied mind; while the hurried step no less marked the tumult of his thoughts. The lamps glittering in the water, which lay below like a dark mirror, recalled him to himself—he was on the very bridge he had crossed in the morning. He was on it, too, alone; not a step broke the silence but his own, and the depths of the shadow which rested on the river, vast and impenetrable, were even as the eternity into which one moment would plunge him. But the skin had taken hold of his imagination. "It is but another four-and-twenty hours, and the experiment will have been fairly tried. We allow to a sick man the indulgence of a whim, why not to a dying one that of his folly?"

So saying, he turned to the lodging of a young friend, whose hospitality he resolved to ask for the night. Scott was at home, and hesitating between a wish for amusement and a fit of idleness—that pleasant idleness which follows indisposition. Never was companion more acceptable: a good fire and a good dinner are very exhilarating—so the two friends were as gay as if there had been no such things as study and suicide in the world. But Charles's spirits were too much those of feverish excitement to last. The jest died upon his lips; Scott's questions were first unanswered, and then unheard: he was only roused from contemplation by confidence.

We again repeat, that there is no temper so communicative as an imaginative one. The poet seems under a necessity of sharing with others the thoughts he has half-created and half-coloured—and among the most reserved of us, who has not experienced, at some time or other, that words had all the relief of tears? One feeling leads to another, in conversation as in everything else; and Charles soon found himself cracking almonds, flinging the shells into the fire, and narrating the whole history of his life.

We shall pass over his childhood more briefly than he did himself—(it is curious how an uncommon position exaggerates our importance in our own eyes)—and take up the thread of the narrative when, at the death of his father, he became "lord of himself, that heritage of wo;"—without money, without a profession, and with relatives on whom he had no claim but kindness—as if that were a claim ever acknowledged by a relative! Not that we would detract one iota from the benevolence which does exist in humanity; there is both more gratitude and more cause for gratitude than it is the fashion now-a-days to admit: but this we do say, that the obligation is never from those on whom we have a claim. Kindness is always unexpected; and "overcomes us like a summer cloud," exciting our "special wonder" as well as thankfulness. In the present state of society, a noble name, without its better part—a noble fortune, is only an encumbrance to its owner. A merely well-born and well-educated young man is the most helpless object in nature. False shame is in him a principle, and the privation of poverty is nothing to its mortification. His habits are opposed to one means of maintenance, his feelings to a second, and his pride to a third. "Dig he cannot, and to beg he is ashamed."

But Charles Smythe had an energy that only required to be thrown upon its own resources, in order to find them. He had literary tastes, and, still more, literary talents; and of all others, these are most conscious of their existence and power. A few weeks saw him established in an upper room in one of those small gloomy streets made for the poor, and in which every city abounds, devoting himself to study and composition, with all the energy of hope, and the delight of present occupation. What a falsehood it is to say that genius and industry are incompatible! Does one work of genius exist that has not also been a work of labour?

"And yet," said Charles, "I cannot describe to you how my heart sunk within me when I first entered the gloomy attic, henceforth destined to be my home, my study, and where so much of my life was to pass. I gazed upon the low ceiling, which seemed to press the air down upon me; a slip of looking-glass, cracked and coarse-grained enough to make you discontented with even yourself, stuck in the plaster; the white-washed walls; the small stove, like that in the cabin of a ship; the wretched little wash-hand stand; the common check furniture of the bed; the parapet before the window—oh, that parapet! I learned afterwards to do justice to the cleanliness of the room—I am not sure, when, in cold weather, I have gone to the extravagance of a handful of fire, whether I have not even thought it comfortable; but to the parapet my eye never became reconciled. In winter the glaring snow lay so piled up on its ledge; in summer it reflected the hot sun like an oven; in rainy weather there the damp seemed to linger:—I do loathe the sight of a parapet! True, that in my father's house there had been, of late years, want of money, confusion, and distress; but still there were the large handsome rooms, there were the servants; and if our guests were few, they had the same speech, dress, and feelings as ourselves. Now I found myself in another world, with which I could not have a word, a hope, an idea, in common.

"Still, I should deceive you, if I told you that after the first week I was miserable. No, my time was fully occupied; I took an intense delight in my pursuits—I was encouraged by small successes—I felt the future was before me: and believe me when I say, that, hopeless, ruined as I am, it is neither the past nor the present which I regret, but the future —that glorious future, to which I once devoted myself— that noblest sacrifice of our nature. I have flung away the immortality of my mind. But remorse is of all feelings the one on which 'vanity of vanities' is written.

"Well, I pursued this course of life for nearly two years; my works had begun to attract some attention; and my relatives, finding I wanted nothing from them, and that I was rather a distinction to them, began to seek me out.

"Going into company purely as a relaxation, I enjoyed it,—to enjoy yourself is the easy method to give enjoyment to others; hence I became popular. My imagination, always on the alert to seek in real life materials for its solitude, flung its interest over every object. I was also lively. What a mistake it is to confound conversational vivacity with good spirits! Few persons who mix in society on the reputation of talent, but feel, or fancy, that there is a necessity for sustaining such reputation: the only method of accomplishing this is by saying something clever, or at least amusing. You know that the many go into the world on the strength of rank or wealth—they have performed their part when they have shewn themselves, their diamonds, or their cashmeres; but you seem to have contracted a debt by your mere admission—and we are all naturally anxious to return an obligation. Soon this exertion for the amusement of others grows a habit—vanity as usual steps in, and then popularity becomes a passion. The worst of it is, the want of moral courage it engenders; you seek too much to say the agreeable instead of the true. Still, this is an excusable fault. Opinion is an author's destiny; what marvel that he should strive by every effort to conciliate an influence so terrible? A despotic power makes slaves.

"This was the pleasantest part of my life. Society relieved without interrupting my studies. I rejoiced in my independence, and was careless about my poverty. I rather disdained than coveted the luxuries I saw: alas! we desire riches more for others than ourselves. What a precious thing would choice be to life! why have we not the sorrowful privilege of rejection? Why, when Laura wished to be introduced to me, did not some interior voice warn me of approaching misery?

"I accompanied to her box the friend who sought me. We entered softly, while Sontag was in the midst of her most popular song, and Mrs. Herbert at first did not perceive us. I stood behind her, admiring the small head, placed so exquisitely on the shoulders; suddenly she turned—I cannot tell you the charm I found in her gentle and somewhat cold manner—the importance of the effect you produced was so much increased by the difficulty there was in discovering its amount. Singularly pale, the marble whiteness of her complexion was strongly contrasted by the black hair, the black dress, and the black drooping feathers of her hat. She well knew the romantic style of her beauty; it was the imagination she sought to interest: hence the young, the enthusiastic, were the victims she selected.

"She said nothing to me of my writings; and I enjoyed the thought that my vanity, at least, had not been enlisted in her favour: I forgot the sweet low voice that so often asked my opinion, the knowledge so unconsciously displayed of my pursuits, and the large black eyes whose every look was a flattery. I have often wondered why she willed to number me among her conquests: but, though I could not give rank or wealth, I could give a name; and, as we always tire of what we do possess, she might desire to exchange the present for the future; the poetry she could not feel, she wished to inspire. Or perhaps, to put it more simply—vanity, like all social vices, craves for novelty; and I had at least the merit of being a stranger. Yet I could not have written a line about her for the world; we write from the memory of love, not its presence. How could I have borne to embody in her image the sorrows which give interest to poetry? If I had been Petrarch, Laura would never have been immortalised in my verse—I should have hated the very glory I myself had created: what, lay my heart bare for the general remark, the common pity! No; the statue I should raise to Love would be like that of Harpocrates, with his finger on his lip.

"In a few days what a gulf opened between my former and present self! I had been content, industrious, devoted to that literature which was at once my hope and my honour. Now, I was idle, restless; I wrote—the pen fell from my hand; I read—the book dropped by my side, and I was lost in some reverie, in which her image was paramount—all my former occupations were at an end; I seemed not to have an idea in the world that did not centre in her.

"All the morning was merged in the moment when, after a thousand of those small disappointments with which 'Circumstance, that unspiritual god,' delights to mock our plans, I perhaps handed her from her carriage to some shop. Every evening was devoted to the chance of meeting her; and, alas! whether I did or did not see her, I turned home with the same sinking of the heart, the same utter depression of spirits.

"For the first time I felt the wide difference between my circumstances and myself. Now, how I coveted riches—how I envied, ay hated, their possessors! Now, how I contrasted the splendid scenes in which I moved with the wretched home where I lived! Now, how worthless seemed all the former landmarks of my ambition!

"God in heaven, how I loved her! I would sit for hours, dreaming all those brilliant impossibilities by which fate might unite our destinies. I placed myself in situations of the most varied interest at her side, and then woke from my phantasy in an agony of shame and regret. The mere mention of her name would make my heart beat even to pain; and yet, with all this inward violence, I was outwardly calm:— true love is like religion, it hath its silence and its sanctity. I felt myself worthy of her, even while I was in reality becoming less so; for the fever of my heart preyed upon my mind, and every hour I was conscious that the power and the glory were departing from me.

"Poetry had been the passion that love now was; but poetry brought forth its fruit in due season: love made all a desert except itself. And yet how slight were the chains that bound me as in fetters of iron! A look, a word, a smile, were the hieroglyphics of the heart, as dazzling to decipher as the characters on

Caliph Vathek's Damascus sabres; and I was blinded like him—indifference and interest were so nicely blended. Now I was chilled by careless coldness—now transported by some slight mark of preference, so slight that only passion could have interpreted it into hope. The very ruin in which my love was involving me, only made it more intense: and ruin, indeed, to me was its engrossment and its idleness.

"Utterly dependent on my own mental exertions, what could I do with my mind such a chaos? Day after day I was importuned to fulfil engagements I had no longer the power of completing. My thoughts, like rebel subjects, disowned my authority—I could concentrate my attention only on one object—Laura. Perhaps the desperation of my circumstances communicated itself to my feelings—I believe Mrs. Herbert feared the passion she had inspired. She shrank from the explanation sudden coldness might have brought on, and tried raillery. Constancy, romance, or enthusiasm, were the recurring objects of her sarcasm.

"One evening, when the large party met at her house had diminished to a small and somewhat confidential group, I remember her saying, as she flung down, disdainfully, a little engraving from a gem—a bird clinging to a leafless bough, with its well-known motto, 'Faithful even unto death'—'Well, fine words are like fine clothes, they make a great deal out of nothing. I often think' (turning to me) 'of the profane speech of the Cardinal, who exclaimed, when he saw the gold and jewels offered at Rome in such profusion by the pious, 'Holy Saints! how profitable has this fable of Christianity been to us!' You poets may well exclaim, 'How profitable has this fable of love been to us!'

"'Ah, madam, you have never loved!' replied a young gentleman, who, like many others of his kind, delighted in talking of what he knew nothing about.

"'Love!' replied she; 'as far as my own experience goes, I do not understand the word: I have never loved. A lover is the personification of weariness; to see the same face, to hear the voice, to separate variety from amusement, in order to centre it all in one—to find a single suffrage sufficient for your vanity. Ah! to love, is in reality the verb the Prussian prince conjugated at Potsdam;' and she sank back on her seat, as if fatigued by the mere recapitulation.

"Notwithstanding her art, Laura was wrong in her calculation. Of all she said I retained only the one delicious phrase, 'I have never loved.' Instead of her indifference, I recalled her beauty, as she leant back on the sofa, one delicate hand balancing her cup, while her perfect figure was half hidden—only to be more gracefully displayed—in a large cloak, which she had drawn round her with the prettiest shiver possible. Day by day my situation became more wretched; one resource alone was left me,—the gaming table; and there a transient success added suspense to my other miseries. "The desire of mortifying a fancied rival, one evening threw unusual softness into Laura's manner; she took my arm, and chance leading us into a small adjacent room, had seated herself on one of the divans before she perceived we were alone. I saw her turn pale and avoid my look; but it was too late,—my heart had found utterance. Scott, I need tell you only her last words,—'And if I did marry, do you think it would be a fortune-hunter?'

"I rose from her feet, and my resolution was taken. I had already sacrificed to Laura my hopes, my principles, my ambition, my fortune; one only sacrifice remained, and that was my life. Still, some remnant of my ancient integrity bade me desire to leave enough behind me to pay my debts. Again I had recourse to the gaming-table; but the fortune which had aided me to evil, deserted me for good: I left the room with a single shilling in my pocket.

"It was long after midnight when I sought my lodgings. The pale, weary look of the girl who opened the door reproached me with my selfish thoughtlessness, in thus, on a cold raw night early in spring, detaining the poor from their needful rest. The mother was by her side, and she appeared far more worn out than the daughter. I have been too engrossed, or I might before have told you of the kindliness of the one, and the surpassing beauty of the other. Now that the image of Ellen Cameron rises before me in all its childish and innocent beauty; when I think of the thousand little acts of kindness—I could almost say tenderness—that escaped from her so unconsciously, I wonder that my heart never took her for its object of imagination and passion. But there is a destiny in all things, and in none more than in love.

"'I shall not detain you long,' said I, as I entered their little parlour. Will you believe me when I say, the uppermost feeling in my mind was distaste at its poor and wretched appearance? The grate smoked, and the thick air was bitter and oppressive to breathe. Drawing the broken china inkstand towards me, I wrote on the back of a letter the assignment of my property (my property!) to Mrs. Cameron. I gave her the paper, and told her that important business forced me to leave London at once; that I could not pay the rent now due, but that the sale of even my few effects would satisfy her claims.

"'You are not going to leave us?' said the woman, on whose memory one or two small services I had rendered her had made a deeper impression than the fear of losing by a lodger so poor as myself. I gave a briefer reply than should have met such kindness, and hurried from the door. As I went down the street, I looked back; Ellen was standing on the steps watching me: she met my eye, and instantly retreated. I caught the last glance of that young and fair face, and felt as if my good angel had deserted me. I passed hastily through the close and narrow streets around my home. Dizzy, confused with the excitement of despair, I was startled by the hour striking one, two, three, four. I was standing before the illuminated clock of St. Bride's. Mockery, thus to trace the progress of time in light! mark it rather by shadows dark and heavy as its own. Half an hour would bring me to Waterloo Bridge, and there I could offer up the fearful sacrifice Fate demanded from Necessity."

From this period we already know the story, and need not follow Charles in his narrative of the small causes which had deterred him from the act, to the wild hope, or rather curiosity, which now induced him to wait for the morrow.

"I have no choice," said he at last; "between myself and the past there is a wide gulf; I cannot again unite quiet industry and enthusiastic energy; I can no longer merge the actual present in the imagined future. A bitter feeling of envy rankles within me. I do not say that there is nothing worth living for, but that there is nothing within my reach. I am weary of this life of literary drudgery, whose toil is so incessant, and whose reward is so distant. I am stung to the very soul by the criticisms on what I have already done. The praise does not gratify me, because it is that of kindness, or of motive, instead of appreciation; the censure mortifies me,—even while I deny its truth; but I say, what is opinion, when the smallest pique against myself, or even my friends—when envy or pure stupidity will turn the balance against me, and withhold from me my so anxiously-sought, my just meed of praise? Again, I feel that youth is rapidly passing, and with it that happiness which youth only can enjoy. What will it avail me, even if future years bring me pleasures for which I no longer care,—pleasures which, if I could command them now, would send the blood through my pulses as if it bore a thousand lives? It is easy to tell me that every lot has its annoyances. I believe nothing which I have not known. Give me the wealth you say has its cares and its vexations; let me try them; let me at least choose my destiny, and then take my chance. Why should I wear out a dreary life in poverty and obscurity, while I loathe the one and despise the other? There are who may talk of calm content, of gliding unnoticed through the road of life; let those who like such ignoble path follow it. Did I make myself? did I wish to enter on this mortal struggle? did I give myself feelings, ideas, or wishes? did I create this difference between myself and my situation? In what am I to blame? Can I help being most unutterably wretched? Tell me not of the benevolence shewn in the organisation of this world; in every part pain and sorrow reign triumphant. True, we are promised a reward hereafter; but that is to depend upon conduct, which it is always difficult, sometimes impossible, to control. My futurity rests upon my belief, as if I could believe what I chose. This is a bad, miserable state,—so bad, that any change must be for the better, at least to me. I cannot go back upon the past; I delude myself no longer. Why should I slave to leave behind me a rich legacy of thought for the careless or ungrateful? A year ago I would not have bartered the world of fame for the world of enjoyment; both are equally beyond me, but I pine now for the latter; and, wanting that, for the calm and the quiet of the cold dark grave. The terrible passion of death is upon me; I long for that eternity which, whether of torture, of annihilation, or of a higher existence, will free me from the intolerable burden of life."

"Two gentlemen to Mr. Smythe," said a servant, opening the door. In one of them Charles recognised the auctioneer. "Ha, ha! young gentleman, come to claim the payment of my bond; this worthy man will soon shew you it is due."

The other, whose solemnity was in singular contrast with the flurry of his companion, now announced himself as Mr. Greaves, solicitor, of Chancery Lane, in whose custody was placed the will of the late Charles Smythe, Esq.

"He was the richest man on 'Change, sir—it's lucky for you that your name is spelt with a y and an e—he made you his heir because you are his namesake: but I have a copy of the will with me, if you please to hear it read." Charles sat bewildered; but his friend Scott, as he was not the heir, retained his senses, and begging them to be seated, poured out a couple of glasses of claret; whereupon the lawyer, after draining one of them, began to read the will, which stated, that "I, Charles Smythe, being of sound mind and body, &c. &c. &c., do will and bequeath to Charles Smythe, my namesake, and, I believe, distant relation (our names being spelt alike), son of, &c. &c., all the property I possess at the time of my decease."

And then followed such a list of estates here, and estates there, mortgages in every county in England, and money vested in the stocks of every known capital—English, French, Russian, and American—that Scott began to think the late Henry Smythe must have been the possessor of Fortunatus's purse. The will was ended, and the little auctioneer could contain himself no longer.

"The luckiest thing in the world that we met to-day! I was in such a fright lest you should have drowned yourself; but I had you watched safe in here—and my boy saw a pie come in; so I thought you'd be sure to live till after dinner. Mr. Greaves has been out hunting for you all day. Lord love you! they're taking on so about you at your lodgings; and Mr. Greaves was afraid you had come to a bad end. Well, he was fagged out when he called on me; and quite down in the mouth to think that a young man should make away with himself just as he came in to such a fine fortune: but I soon heartened him up. We had a beef-steak together, and then came off here: glad to find you alive and merry."

Scott could not restrain his laughter; but Charles sat gloomily folding and unfolding the skin of shagreen, which he had taken from his pocket.

"I must say good night," said the solicitor, who had just finished the last glass of claret; "I keep regular hours—always at home by twelve, and have a long way to go. I will call on you to-morrow—ten o'clock precisely—Mr. Smythe: we have not a little business to settle. Good night!"

"And good night, gentlemen," added the auctioneer; and then, addressing Charles more particularly, "I have a large amount to make up by the 15th of this month, so hope you won't forget our little account. I am sure you won't grudge the money, considering the luck the skin has brought you. Wish you joy of your good fortune!"

"And I wish," exclaimed Charles, "that you may break your neck going down stairs."

This kind farewell was, however, lost on its object, who had just closed the door.

"What a lucky fellow you are! I congratulate you from my heart," said Scott.

"This accursed skin!" exclaimed Charles.

"Why, you are not silly enough to think that has any thing to do with it! By the by, how shamefully that rascally auctioneer has taken you in! He knew of the will beforehand, and has played nicely upon your excited state of mind. I hope you mean to dispute the payment of the bond?"

A loud noise in the passage interrupted their conversation.

They say gravity is the centre of attraction; I rather think that noise is. Nothing so soon assembles the inhabitants of a house as a loud and sudden noise: it did so in the present instance.

"For the love of God, run for a surgeon; he is quite senseless!" And the first thing the friends saw was Mr. Greaves and the servant raising the body of the auctioneer.

Charles, faint and trembling, grasped the bannisters: Scott sprang forward.

"The whole College of Physicians can do him no good: he has broken his neck!"

"Do you now doubt," exclaimed Charles, "my fatal power? Behold how, within the last minute, the skin has shrunk!"

"Your good luck has turned your brain. I advise you to go home, and be bled and blistered," said Scott. "The broken neck of the auctioneer is just an unlucky coincidence."

"It is my terrible destiny!" cried Charles Smythe.

Wealth, wealth unbounded, and which every day some lucky chance served to increase, was now in Charles Smythe's possession—he had all of pleasure, all of luxury, excepting their enjoyment; for the weight was on his spirits, and the worm at his heart. His slightest wish was invariably accomplished; but at every wish the skin of shagreen diminished, and with it he felt his health and strength decline. He found he had but one reserve—to desire nothing. Gradually his splendid abode became a solitude, and his habits those of an ascetic. He ate before he was hungry, lest he should wish for food; he slept with his night-draught drugged with laudanum, lest he should crave repose.

Once, and once only, he met Laura. He turned from her with loathing: was not she the cause of his present doom? Mrs. Herbert marked his avoidance with a sweet laugh and a stinging jest:—"So much for a romantic attachment! My poet-lover has not a guinea in the world, and he vows eternal constancy aux beaux yeux de ma cassette. He becomes a millionaire, and nous avons changé tout cela—the passionate and the elevated degenerates into the indifferent and the calculating. Never tell me of disinterested love!"

There was perhaps some bitterness in this; but when was a woman ever witty without being bitter? Think for a moment how her feelings must have been frozen before they could sparkle, and how their edge must have been ground down before they became so keen: brilliant and caustic words are but the outward type of that which is within.

"I will consult a physician to-morrow," said Charles Smythe one night, after he had spent about an hour in gazing alternately on his pale and altered face in the glass, and then on the skin of shagreen now most wofully diminished.

Next morning saw his carriage at Dr. Thomson's door. He was shewn into a back room, fitted up as a study. Large and learned volumes lined the sides; above the fire-place stood a row of glass phials, each containing a snake, a frog, or a lizard, preserved in spirits of wine; and on the table lay open a huge portfolio of ghastly-looking prints. Somehow or other, it was a room that gave you great confidence in your doctor:—you thought, what a clever man he must be! The patient now entered on his history. At its finish, the physician no longer restrained his reassuring smile—"I will give you my advice, though I very much doubt your taking it: enlist for six months in any marching regiment you can find, and permit me to throw this piece of shagreen behind the fire."

So saying, he took up the talisman, and was about to suit the action to the word, when Charles snatched it from him with a piercing cry, and rushed out of the house. He then directed his coachman to drive to Sir Henry Halford's. He was shewn into an elegant drawing-room; a large glass reflected the crimson colour flung on his countenance by the curtains: it was a very reviving shade. Again the patient began his narrative, which was listened to this time with the most touching attention. Sir Henry took his hand with an air of almost affectionate interest—said something about over-excitement, nerves, and genius— wrote a prescription—advised quiet and country air. "Take some pretty place, quite retired, but near enough to town for a morning's drive to bring you to London; for I must see you again—not often, I hope;—not often, I am sure!" muttered the physician, as his patient withdrew.

Charles Smythe now resolved on taking a place in the country; but he equally resolved on wishing nothing about it. He would drive a few miles out of town, and take the first place to let that he liked. The horses baited at a small country inn; he had lunched; and then, for fear he might get weary, and wish for a stroll, he wandered out. It was an unusually hot day, in an unusually forward spring; but the sunshine was cheerful, and the heat was softened by the wide and leafy branches of the elm-trees whose boughs met overhead. The hedges were covered with May, in the fragile and fragrant luxuriance of its short-lived blossom. On each side were meadows of deep grass, now of a dark and shadowy, now of a bright and glittering green, as the sunbeam or the cloud passed alternately over them. A low but pleasant murmur, the whisper of leaves, the chirrup of the birds, the stir of insect wings, was on the air; and as the invalid wound down the green lane, he forgot for a while how rich and how wretched he was. His thoughts wandered in as desultory a manner as he did himself, fixing rather on objects without than within. He was roused from his reverie by that sudden rustling among the boughs which tells the approach of a summer shower. The light branches of the ash were tossed aside by the wind, and a few heavy drops fell almost one by one. A large black cloud darkened the sky, and a burst of distant thunder rolled upon the air.

"To be caught in the rain will give me my death of cold," exclaimed Charles, almost unconsciously hurrying forward. For a moment he hesitated whether he should not wish the rain to cease; but the remedy was worse than the disease—so on he went. Luckily, a sudden turn in the lane shewed him a place of shelter; he soon reached the stone porch of a small cottage, and paused there, gaining breath and resolution to ask admission. Built in a heavy Gothic style of architecture, the cottage looked as if it had formerly been the lodge of some park. In one of the windows sat a girl: her head was bent on her hand, and her fair hair, simply parted on the forehead, was covered by a square cap, or rather coif. Surely he knew her face! She looked up, and their eyes met; another instant, and the door stood open;—it was Ellen Cameron! Such a smile and such a blush, such a beautiful agitation as that with which he was welcomed! She recognised him at the first glance, as he did her at the second.

"My mother will be so glad to see you!" was her exclamation; and he was shewn into the prettiest little room that ever was crowded with flowers, or opened into a garden whose roses looked in at the window. There her mother was sitting; and Charles was touched (how could he be otherwise?) by the earnest and simple delight of his welcome.

Their history was soon told. Mrs. Cameron's lawsuit had been decided in her favour, and their present competency was rendered more delicious by past poverty. They had immediately left London; and this accounted for Charles's not having been able to find them out when he made the endeavour, which, in justice to his gratitude, we ought to mention he had done.

"Your books are quite safe," said Mrs. Cameron, "and so is your writing-table; but they are in Ellen's room, for she is a great reader."

Ellen blushed to the temples. Their visitor smiled when he remembered how little his learned and ponderous tomes were likely to interest the young and fair creature who had them in her care.

Charles Smythe was pressed to stay dinner. He consented; and the day passed pleasantly enough to make him say, towards evening, "I wish I could find a house to suit me." The words "I wish" struck upon his heart with a cold chill, which was forgotten as he thought how very lovely the flush of delight made Ellen's always beautiful face.

We will omit the love-making, as it must be personal to be pleasant; and come to the conclusion, which every reader can by this time foresee, viz. matrimony. The bright and buoyant month of June, the brightest of all our year, witnessed Charles Smythe's marriage. The bells were yet ringing a joyous peal, softened by the distance into music, as he stood with a folded paper in his hand by a small ebon escritoire. "Why," said he, "should I be weak enough to allow a vain delusion to prey upon my spirits and wear away my health? No doubt being exposed to the open air shrinks up the skin: for three months I will not look at it." He locked the drawer, and turned to meet his beautiful bride, whose light step now entered the room.

To use the established phrase, three months of uninterrupted happiness glided away—a phrase, though in frequent use, whose accuracy I greatly doubt; there being no such thing as uninterrupted happiness any how or any where. But one morning, while wandering through the shadowy walks with which his gardens abounded, he heard the voices of his wife and her mother. He looked through the boughs, for one moment, on the fair and young face whose beauty was so precious in his eyes—so precious, for he felt how entirely it was his own. There was something at once womanly and childish in Ellen's love for her husband—womanly in its devotion, childish in its implicit reliance—one of those worshipping, exaggerating, uplooking attachments which it is so satisfactory to man's vanity to inspire. But an expression of strong anxiety was on her face, and her cheek was very pale. Charles was just about to step forward and kiss it into colour, when the sound of his own name arrested his advance.

"I would not, dearest, alarm you unnecessarily," said Mrs. Cameron; "but you must make Charles have medical advice: he looks wretchedly ill, and grows worse every day."

He saw Ellen start, as if first awakened to the terrible consciousness of her husband's ill health—he saw her bow her face on her hands in an agony of tears; but he staid not to console her—his heart was hardened by the fear of death. "I have been married three months to-day; I will go and look at the skin of shagreen." While unlocking the writing-case in which it lay, he caught sight of his shadow in a glass opposite: he beheld, as it were, the spectre of himself. Shuddering, he hurriedly opened the drawer. "The skin of shagreen is not here!" exclaimed he—and sank on the sofa breathless with delight. The fatal skin had disappeared, and yet he lived! "Fool, fool that I have been, to allow a nameless dread to poison my food, to fever my sleep! Ellen, my sweet Ellen, we shall be happy yet!" The remembrance of her sorrow rose to his mind.

No longer stern and selfish with a gloomy dread, he opened the window; to cross the turf would bring him to her side immediately. The wind swept through the casement, and blew the papers, &c. to his feet. He turned pale, his eyes swam; every other object was indistinct, for uppermost of all lay the skin of shagreen; but so small, no wonder he had overlooked it—it was the size of a willow-leaf, fragile and withered as they are with the first frost! How prodigal of life had the last three months been!—not the slightest wish of Ellen's but had found an echo in his! Why, the mere hope that a summer-day would not bring premature destruction to a half-blown rose—even such light words were those of the grave! What was Ellen's self but a beautiful death?

Again every faculty was absorbed in a passionate longing for life—life under any circumstances. He left his home on the instant; wrote from London, that pressing business took him abroad for some time; and in the course of a week he was settled in a solitary cottage at Clifton. Here his days passed in a melancholy monotony; he rose at the same hour, took a long walk, dined, walked again, and then slept. He read no books, he saw no friends, he had no wish but for life; and night after night he examined the frail remnant of shagreen, and as often found it undiminished. At this rate he might live for years—and his heart leaped for joy at the thought of this dull and unnatural existence. Youth, wealth, fame, love, had all merged in the dread of death.

It was a fine soft evening in September, when he leant, as was his wont, in an arm-chair by the window, watching with fixed but languid gaze the deep shadows of the trees, while every open space was silver with the light of the moon—the hunter's moon, as the large bright orb of that month is called. The garden was close to the road, and the step and voice of the few passers-by were distinctly heard. Suddenly one went along singing: it was a young voice, but both air and words were sad. Charles caught the first verse:—

O leave me to my sorrow,
    For my heart is oppress'd to-day!

O leave me, and to-morrow
  Dark clouds will have pass'd away!

The song died in the distance; not so in the heart of the recluse. "I may," said the miserable slave of himself, "be left to my sorrow; but when will my dark clouds pass away? Never till they deepen into the night of death! Buoyant and reckless spirit of my youth, all ye thousand hopes that bore me up as with the wings of an eagle, where are ye now? The knowledge I acquired, the fame for which I burned, the wealth I so coveted—all mine, yet not mine! And must all that makes life desirable be purchased but by the loss of life? Is this the secret of existence? At what a price of wretchedness must even this miserable and monotonous life be bought! My poor Ellen, what must my absence seem to her!"

As the image of his young and deserted wife rose before him in all its gentle beauty, a gush of tenderness softened him for the moment. "My sweet Ellen!" exclaimed he, almost unconsciously, "would to God you were here!"

"Ah, now I dare speak to you!" whispered a sweet low voice.

Love was mightier than fear; and happy as herself, he kissed away the tears that fell thick and fast from the sweet eyes raised so timidly to his own.

"How could you leave me? who would watch over you with affection like mine?"

At these words he started from his seat, and snatched the skin of shagreen—it was reduced to a mere shred. "Ellen," exclaimed he, grasping her arm, "do you see this accursed thing? it is my life; one other wish is my death-warrant!"

He looked on the ghastly terror which marked his wife's features; his heart misgave him for her agony; and again, almost unwittingly, he wished her fear might cease! A deadly pain rushed over him, his eyes closed even on that beloved countenance; he strove to speak, the words died in an inarticulate murmur; a frightful convulsion distorted his face as it sank on Ellen's shoulder;—his last breath and the skin of shagreen had passed away together!

THE KNIFE

What a pretty, fair, delicate-looking girl was Harriet Lynn! how well I remember her, with her small black silk bonnet, casting a deeper shadow on the light-brown hair that escaped in waves rather than curls from the bondage of her cap; the neat white handkerchief, the dark stuff dress, the full sleeves a little turned back from the slender wrist, and hands whose softness had been uninjured by their ordinary employment—that of plaiting the finest straw. Many a summer's evening have I seen her stand at the gate of the cottage-garden, over which hung a cherry-tree, the pride of her uncle; indeed, rather a source of congratulation to the village at large, so much was its size and fertility admired by strangers— so beautiful in spring, with its avalanche of white blossom—so rich in summer, with its multitude of crimson berries. There would Harriet stand, the shining straws passing with rapidity through her slight fingers; with a gentle smile and a kind word for all those passers-by whom she knew, and a deep blush and sudden attention to her work for all whom she knew not. Harriet was not a native of our part of the country; her parents' death had thrown her on the kindness of an uncle and aunt, who, having no child of their own, were happy to adopt her. Some little roughness in that course which is said never to run smooth—very true love—would seem to be the worst history that could be connected with the pretty peasant. But not so: her arrival in our county was attended by one of those terrible incidents which make humanity shudder at itself, and which are awful in proportion to their rareness. It is taking nature in the worst possible point of view, to think that custom reconciles even to crime.

It was a sad morning when Harriet Lynn left her native village: she rose long before the appointed time. When at the stile by the beech-tree, she was to be taken up by John Dodd the carrier, who often gave a neighbour a lift to the next town. This stile was at the entrance of the churchyard—a sorrowful resting-place to one whose nearest and dearest were yet scarce cold in their tomb. Ever and anon did she enter and seek the far corner, where, beneath the shadow of an old yew-tree, was a grave: it held two tenants—they were her father and her mother, and she looked now on their place of rest for the last time. There is a strange mixture in our feelings; perhaps the consciousness that all her earnings had gone towards erecting the stone whose white surface bore the names of her parents, mingled a little satisfaction with her grief: and why should it not? The discharge of a duty from affection is the best solace for sorrow.

At length the cart appeared at some distance on the winding road; and in a few minutes Harriet Lynn began a journey, of whose length and difficulties she had the usually exaggerated notion of all young travellers. The gallantry of an English peasant rarely expands into words. John Dodd received her with a good-natured grin, and pushed on his way—for he was carrier of Donnington and some dozen parishes round; at each of which he duly deposited at least a score of packages or messages. His first pause was at a small shop situated on the east side of Donnington moor.

"None so deaf as those who won't hear. Now this plaguy old woman will keep me bawling for an hour; it's always so when I'm in a hurry."

Sure enough his vociferations obtained no answer; so, asking his companion to hold the reins, while he went to see if Dame Bird were dead or asleep, he jumped out of the cart, taking with him sundry square brown-paper parcels, from whose contents the various odours of tea, sugar, and tallow exhaled. The little garden gate was, as usual, open; and the first thing that struck the carrier was a quantity of currants trampled upon the brick walk,

"Somebody's pudding will be none the better for this; but it's a wonder the old woman has not been out broom in hand. I say, Dame Bird! you might sell your currants over again—none the worse for a little clean dirt."

At this moment he started back, with open eyes and gaping mouth:—what an odd thing it is, that the indications of terror are usually ludicrous! A narrow crimson line, like the wriggling of a red snake, wound slowly towards him: it was blood! For the first time in his life, John Dodd dropped a parcel from his hand, and ran into the shop. The narrow line widened; large red spots grew frequent; the crimson pool splashed beneath his feet—it evidently flowed from behind the counter; and there lay the poor old woman, her face uppermost, and her throat literally cut from ear to ear.

"Murder! thieves! Harriet Lynn, help!" cried the terrified carrier, rushing back to his cart and companion, as if even the girl and his horse were some security.

Harriet Lynn, who had heard his voice, was at the gate as soon as himself.

"What is the matter?"

"Come away; we shall be murdered!" was the answer, made almost inaudible by dread.

There is no denying the fact, that in all sudden emergencies a woman has ten times the presence of mind, or, to use the common expression, her wits more about her than a man. Harriet Lynn turned white as the ghastly idea suggested itself; but she proceeded to the shop, followed by her companion, who thought that as she went, he must go too. The sight was too fearful; and for a moment she walked again into the garden, till the fresh air restored her from her feeling of deadly sickness. Perhaps the distinction between the two witnesses was, that in the girl horror was the predominant sensation, while in the man it was terror.

"There is no likelihood of the murderer having hidden himself here; however, we must see." And she resolutely returned to the house.

Fright had quite paralysed John Dodd's faculties, and he went after her mechanically. The cottage was only one story high, and the small room behind the shop was where the old woman slept. Marks of violence were visible in every part; a cupboard had been forced open, and the contents of a chest of drawers were scattered about the room. The shop bore even more evident signs of spoliation—that reckless wastefulness which seems the constant companion of cruelty; but little of the grocery appeared to have been touched, excepting the sweet things.

"We must go," said Harriet, "and get assistance as fast as we can. Is Mr. March still our justice?"

The proposal of leaving was very welcome to the carrier, who expected every minute to be murdered too. Yet, Harriet would not leave till the shutters were barred and the door locked: the large key hung as usual behind it, and that she took with her. "No one can now get either in or out."

They drove with all possible speed to Mr. March's, where they had instant admission. John Dodd had not yet recovered his senses; but his companion's account was equally brief and clear. A messenger was forthwith despatched to the coroner, then at Newcastle, where the assizes were holding, about five miles distant: and Mr. March proceeded to the cottage, of which Harriet Lynn gave him the key. Being on horseback, he, and two neighbours who accompanied him, arrived at the place long before their train of curious and horror-stricken followers. They found everything as had been described. The body was in a frightful state; the hands and arms of the poor old creature were covered with gashes; and a violent blow on the temple had probably occasioned her fall and stunned her, for the throat was cut with a degree of neatness and precision, which shewed that then at least the victim could not have struggled. Close to the corpse was found a small tortoise-shell penknife clotted with blood, evidently the instrument by which the wound had been inflicted. Neighbours now came hurrying in, and one after another missed some trifling article of property which the deceased was known to have possessed. There were three thin spoons, real silver, on which she greatly prided herself; they were gone. A large silver watch, together with a red silk shawl and a Bandana handkerchief, very regular parts of her Sunday attire, were also not to be found.

After the first burst of dismay was over, two subjects were universally started as topics of conversation; first, how everyone had predicted that "a poor lone woman" was sure to be murdered; and, secondly, as to "who was the murderer?" Here there was an unusual coincidence of opinion. A gipsy and his wife had for the last week been in the neighbourhood, and their presence had been testified by innumerable small thefts. The man was dogged and sullen, apparently without occupation or motive for staying among them; the woman pretty, active, and with a great gift of fortune-telling. Many recollected seeing them both prowling about the little shop; and some, who came in last, stated that their encampment by the nut-tree wood was deserted. After the coroner's inquest, suspicion was sufficiently roused for a warrant to be issued for the apprehension of the prisoners. They were overtaken in a by-lane some miles distant, and brought to Newcastle, vehemently protesting their innocence.

The female was first examined. She evidently required to have the questions put to her in the simplest form, otherwise, from her imperfect knowledge of the English tongue, she could not comprehend them. All her replies were as simple as they were straight-forward. She was powerfully affected when the magistrate spoke to her of the cruelty of the deed; but it was, or seemed to be, a natural and womanly horror of so shocking a crime. Nothing could be elicited from her that excited suspicion; on the contrary, the effect she produced was a very favourable one.

It now came to the gipsy's own turn. Fierceness, defiance, and a shrewd and bold speech, characterised his answers. He was asked why he came into that part of the country?

"Because it is one of the very few places where there is a patch of green grass and an old tree whose shelter may be had without payment."

He was then interrogated—"Why, having such an advantage, he had abandoned it?"

"Because my habits are not as your habits. You dwell in houses, as if you were like the stock or the stone with which they are built; I wander as free and as far as the wind. Look ye! our faces are not as your faces, our speech is not as your speech; we have come from a distant country, over seas and mountains, over rough paths and smooth roads; we have numbered more miles than your whole island contains; and yet you ask us why we left one little village! I left it because it was my will to do so."

The pack which each carried was examined; and though convincing proofs of divers small thefts appeared, nothing was found that had been Mrs. Bird's property. Still, the general feeling was so strong against them, that they were committed for trial, which took place the following week.

Death never excites such sympathy as it does when it assumes the shape of murder. In a few days the little garden was stripped of every plant, rosemary, rue, currant, and gooseberry bush, potato and cabbage,—all that their possessors might have some relic of "the horrible murder;" and every one planted the spoil in the most conspicuous part of their own garden. The poor old woman had been universally liked; she had kept that shop forty years; nothing had induced her to leave it, though the original motive for settling there had long passed away. The "Great House," as it was wont to be called, where she had lived servant, and which had once been scarcely twice a stone's throw from her home, had since been pulled down. Mrs. Bird had for many years been the sole chronicler of the glories of "the old family;" and her former connexion with it gave her still something of consequence in the eyes of her neighbours. The most scrupulous honesty, a cheerful temper, and a great love for children (a singularly popular quality), a regular attendance at church (on fine Sundays in the bright red shawl, on wet ones in a less bright red cloak), and a naturally good understanding, made her beloved, and her advice often both asked and taken. Many complained of the distance of her shop, but no one thought of going to another. All respected the feeling that made the old woman cling to the spot which had witnessed her youth, her marriage, and her old age. She had wedded, early in life, one of the gardeners of the "Great

House," who, to use that common but most expressive phrase, had turned out "no better than he should do." Luckily, going home one night in a state of intoxication, he broke his neck—an event Mrs. Bird deplored much more than her neighbours thought necessary. However, it was not that sort of grief which requires consolation; and the widow was not tempted to forget the miseries of her first marriage in the happiness of a second. She never gave hope that triumph over experience, which Dr. Johnson so ungallantly declares a second wedding to be. Years after years rolled away, and Mrs. Bird and her shop seemed as much part of the moor as the stunted furze-bushes. No one dreamt of change till the morning of the murder, and then, as we have said, every body had foreseen what the old woman's living by herself, in such an out-of-the-way place, would come to.

Human nature is accused of much more selfishness than it really has; a thousand kindly emotions break in upon and redeem our daily and interested life. As Wordsworth beautifully says—

"The poorest poor
Long for some moments in a weary life,
When they can know and feel that they have been
Themselves the fathers and the dealers out
Of some small blessings—have been kind to such
As needed kindness; for this single cause.
That we have all of us one human heart."

And this old and solitary woman had been the rallying point for much good feeling, evinced in numerous little acts of common service. Many a young girl would give an hour's time to the sewing and darning to which Mrs. Bird's eyes were no longer equal—many a neighbour rose somewhat earlier to help her in her garden; and not a creature went to or from market without pausing for a few minutes with the "poor soul who must be so lonely." Nor was the old dame without her kindness and her favours to bestow in return. She had more than once accommodated a friend with a humble, but most serviceable loan; and would rather give very dubious credit for sugar and raisins at Christmas, than "that the poor children should go without their bit of plum-pudding once a-year." She was learned in decocting all kinds of herb-tea, infallible in curing burns, sprains, and scalds; and not a few pennyworths of gingerbread and paradise (for the latter she was very famous) went among her young customers, for which the till was never the richer. No wonder, therefore, that her most barbarous murder exasperated the peasantry almost to frenzy against the supposed criminals.

On the examination of the gipsies, nothing had been elicited from either in the slightest degree corroborative of the charge against them. The man was at first furious, struggled with the officers, boldly declared his innocence, and finally settled down into sullen silence. The woman was quiet and gentle, watching only her husband's eye, and confirming all his assertions. The prisoners attracted great attention; they were both singular and superior, evidently very different from the ignorant and simple villagers among whom they ordinarily moved. Rachel (such was the female's name) was perfectly beautiful, though in the peculiar style which belongs to her race: delicately made, with a mild and mournful cast of countenance, she seemed the last person in the world to have engaged in an act of violence; indeed, the most distant allusion to the murder drove the colour from her dark cheek, and convulsed her slight frame with a shudder of fear and loathing. There was something very remarkable in her devotion to her husband; it was a mixture of deference, tenderness, and submission. Her age appeared to be about twenty; and a general and strong sympathy was excited for a creature so young, so lovely, and so meek.

The man was obviously turned of forty; his black hair was mixed with gray, and the fine outline of his features was harsh with time and exposure to all weathers. He was tall, and his gait even commanding; his hands and feet were of that small and fine mould we are accustomed to attribute to gentle blood; the expression of his face was one which spoke both intellect and courage, though still more ferocity: he seemed to belong to some other time than the present, when human life was held but lightly, and when a shrewder wit or a stronger arm made man a chief among his fellow-savages.

We have seen that nothing was elicited on their examination. Still, taking all that could be discovered into consideration—first, that they had been observed speaking to the old woman the day before; secondly, the approximation of their encampment to the shop—for their tent was pitched in a small hazel-wood copse not a quarter of a mile distant from the place; thirdly, their abrupt departure; and, fourthly, that not a shadow of suspicion could attach to any but themselves:—on these grounds, as already mentioned, they had been ordered to be committed for trial to the county gaol. It was not till the female found she was to be parted from her husband (for each was, of course, to be confined in a separate cell) that she uttered a cry, or made a gesture of resistance: then, even the gaolers were touched by the passionate despair with which she clung to his knees, and implored him to let her remain, as if it depended solely on his will. His only answer consisted in holding out to her his manacled hands. It became necessary to separate them by force. Just as they bore her to the threshold, the gipsy suddenly asked permission to bid her farewell: he advanced towards her, and said something in a low voice and in a foreign tongue. Her struggles ceased; she made a brief reply in the same language, raised her hands with a very peculiar gesture above her head, and then pressed them to her heart. A look passed between them, and she was led quietly from the room.

During the week of her imprisonment, her humble and sad bearing won upon the hearts of all. The elderly clergyman exerted even more than his usual anxious care; but the holy eloquence which had subdued so many a sinner to repentance, and worked good out of evil, here utterly failed. The blessed truths of the Christian faith were poured fruitlessly into ears that evidently heard them for the first time, and were lost upon one whose belief was already given to the wild superstitions taught in childhood and youth. It was equally vain to question her about the crime for which they were committed to prison; her constant reply was, "He said he was innocent: why do you doubt him?"

Once and once only did she ask after her companion, and then instantly checked herself; more, it seemed, from a fear of giving him offence, than out of any regard to those around her. There was a singular character about the love she manifested towards him; it united the passionate devotedness of the mistress, the entire union of interests felt by the wife, the submission of the child, and something of the awe and homage paid by the vassal to his master. The gipsy's own conduct had been very different; he had contrived to make himself an object of fear and hate to every one who had approached him. But his fierce, sullen temper, and his great natural gifts, combined with a degree of knowledge surprising in his station, were principally called forth in his interviews with the clergyman, whose arguments were met either by ingenious sophistries and turned aside from their real meaning, or by vindictive reproaches and keen and bitter sneers. With regard to the crime, he never swerved from his assertion of innocence.

At length the day of trial arrived. Assuredly the English trial for murder is an awful assembling; the vague look of serious horror, which would be ludicrous under any other circumstances, is here redeemed by its fearful source. The grave costume of the bar, the dignified solemnity of the judge, the long robes, all differing from the ordinary apparel of daily life, have their full effect on at least two thirds of the spectators. Some may be too thoughtful, others too thoughtless, to have their imagination affected by all this "pomp of circumstance;" but this is far from being the feeling of the generality.

The court was crowded at an unusually early hour. Gradually the dense and silent mass gave way before the slow approach of the judge: he took his seat; the twelve jurymen followed—there was a slight stir as each one settled in his place, and then all was quiet as the grave.

There is a deep impression of awe produced by such a vast but silent crowd; we are at once conscious that the cause is terrible which can induce the unusual stillness. The issue of a trial on which hangs life or death, is indeed an appalling thing. We know that men are about to take away that which they cannot give—that a few words of human breath will deprive of breath one of the number for ever; and though we acknowledge that in this evil world punishment is the only security against crime, and that blood for blood has been a necessity from the beginning of time; still, we feel that the necessity is a dreadful one. A low murmur of execration—something like the dull sound of the sea, when the waves prophesy, as it were, of the coming storm—ran through the court as the prisoners were brought in.

"Order!" said the judge, in a clear, calm voice; and again the deepest stillness prevailed. The female came first, so wrapped in her cloak that both her face and figure were quite concealed. The gipsy himself advanced with as much indifference, and casting as careless glances around, as if he were but walking over a wild heath on a summer morning. He was dressed in a loose great-coat, fastened about his waist with a leathern belt, and wore round his throat a dingy crimson handkerchief; yet, in spite of his dress, he had that air of dignity which personal advantages always confer when attended by entire freedom and self-possession. His height, his firm step, his handsome features, attracted every one; but not an eye met his without shrinking from its keen and ferocious expression:—not a single individual present thought him innocent.

Both were placed at the bar; and on a sign from the judge, the officer at her side removed the muffling from the female prisoner's face: she appeared scarcely conscious of the action. The long black hair, utterly unconfined, fell down in a mass of dark ringlets, strongly contrasted by the bright red cloak; they hung back off the countenance, whose sweet and childish beauty was thus fully displayed. She had the small smooth features, the fresh colour, the unconscious smile, which belongs only to very early youth, and those large, soft, beseeching eyes with which we almost unawares connect the idea of helplessness and innocence. It was like sacrilege to Nature to suspect of crime a creature so lovely. Those opposite could observe that her whole attention was fixed on a beautiful nosegay placed on the bench near the judge. The season was too far advanced for the gardens to boast much bloom; and the rich bunch of purple and crimson flowers was from the hot-house of a gentleman noted for his rare collection of tropical plants. Her eyes filled with tears—was it possible that the spicy perfume and magnificent dyes of the bouquet before her recalled the associations of her childhood?

The prisoners were now required to plead guilty or not guilty. "Not guilty!" replied the gipsy, with an air of mingled confidence and defiance.

His wife had not till that moment been aware of his presence. At the first tone of his voice, she sprang forward with a cry and look of intense delight, and throwing herself at his feet, embraced his knees, while joy and affection found vent in a passionate burst of tears. The gipsy seemed the least moved of any by the touching love of his wife; he rather suffered than returned her caresses, receiving them more as homage is accepted, than as fondness is requited.

How incomprehensible is woman's love!—it is not kindness that wins it, nor return that insures it; we daily see the most devoted attachment lavished on those who seem to us singularly unworthy. The Spectator shewed his usual knowledge of human nature, when, in speaking on this subject, he relates, that in a town besieged by the enemy, on the women being allowed to depart with whatever they held most precious, only one among them carried off her husband,—a man notorious for his tyrannical temper, and who had, moreover, a bad—or, as it turned out, a good—habit of beating his wife every morning. Well, all governments are maintained by fear—fear being our great principle of action; and fear, we are tempted to believe, heightens and strengthens the love of woman.

For a minute, even the judge interfered not with a display of emotion so earnest and so affecting; and before the officers approached to separate the prisoners, Rachel arose at her husband's bidding, and stood quietly and meekly at his side.

John Dodd, the first witness examined, contrived to throw into his story the confusion of his own ideas. Harriet Lynn came next, and was just as remarkable for the simplicity and clearness of her answers. Still, their evidence only proved the fact of the murder, not by whom it had been committed.

The fearless make their own way—and the male prisoner's bold bearing was not without its effect. The tide of opinion turned rapidly in his favour; people began to think that a man might have a profusion of black elf-like locks and a ferocious expression of countenance, and yet not be an actual murderer.

But we must go back to a period a little previous to the trial.

Among the barristers who went the northern circuit was a Mr. Harvey, as shrewd a counsel as had ever merged a life-time in law, save a few youthful reminiscences, which his compeers called folly, but to which, nevertheless, they themselves turned with great satisfaction. Mr. Harvey's birthplace was within a few miles of Newcastle, where he always arrived one day before the assizes commenced; which day was as invariably spent in riding about the country, visiting all his boyish haunts, and ended by a dinner with two or three old friends, at the same inn, where he had now regularly dined for the last twenty years. It was one of those beautiful days with which October abounds more than any other month; a soft west-wind expanded the few late flowers that yet made glad the more sheltered nooks; the oaks, beeches, and chestnuts (for the country was densely wooded), still wore their richest and darkest green; while the limes and sycamores contrasted them strongly with their bright red and vivid yellow. Haymaking and harvest had long been over; so that little of rustic employment remained in the fields, whose stillness was almost unbroken.

Now and then, as Mr. Harvey rode slowly along scenes so familiar to him, he was startled from his reverie by the sudden rise of a covey of birds in an adjacent field; or, in passing a secluded copse, the glossy plumage of the pheasant caught his eye, while the air was stirring with the sound of its loud and peculiar flight; and sometimes, faint and echoing in the distance, came the report of the solitary sportsman's gun, "few and far between."

It was in a little lonely lane, girded on one side by a thick wood almost entirely composed of young oaks, and on the other by a grass-field and then a garden, both belonging to a small farmhouse. There was an aspect of comfort and neatness, which spoke well for the inhabitants; a pear-tree covered the front that faced the road, and the porch was overgrown with Chinese roses, so delicate-looking, yet so hardy. Two children were standing close to the hedge, and their conversation accidentally caught Mr. Harvey's attention, who was riding along at that sauntering pace for which a green and shadowy lane seems especially made.

"Ah! grandfather will never bring you anything again; I've got his scissors quite safe."

So saying, the little girl held up, with a great air of triumph, a shining pair of those feminine weapons, dangling by a piece of blue riband to her waist.

"I'll tell him all about it; and I shall be the favourite then, and not you, Master Jem."

"I'm sure, Mary," said the boy, "you need'nt talk; didn't I give you the string of birds' eggs I got for it?"

"Well, well," replied his tormentor, who seemed about nine—a year older than her brother, "a knife cuts love, they say; and your grandfather won't love you no more, now you've sold the knife he gave you. I've got my scissors—I've got my scissors! and you've sold your penknife—your pretty tortoise-shell penknife!"

And the girl ran down the garden, singing her last words over and over, her brother following, with a look half of remorse and half of anger.

"Born with them—born with them: all alike! No pleasure equal to the pleasure of tormenting, to a woman. Well, my little maiden, some ten years hence your brother will not be the only person you'll plague."

So saying, the lawyer pushed his horse into a sort of discontented trot.

A brisk ride, however, was exceedingly beneficial; and both he and his friends did full justice to the fresh trout and small mutton, which, for a score of years, the same landlord had prepared, and the same guests partaken of, at the White Hart. After dinner they gathered round the large, bright coal fire, whose one neatly-cut log emitted a shower of sparkles at every touch of the poker,—talked of former times,— sipped some fine old port, with a cobweb dress as fragile and more precious than any blonde veil Chantilly ever produced,—and felt more and more convinced, that though the world was a very bad one, yet there were some few things in it worth living for.

All recollection of the children and of their conversation had faded from Mr. Harvey's memory; but when a small tortoise-shell penknife was produced on the trial,—with that cultivated acuteness which formed so large a part both of his natural and acquired character, the coincidence instantly struck him. He was not engaged on either side; so, leaving the court, he drove with all rapidity to the farm in the green and lonely lane. It was about five miles distant. The farmer was at home, and the barrister soon explained both his business and his plan. The child was sent for—a little, frank, bold-looking boy, of eight years old.

"So, my fine fellow," said Mr. Harvey, "you sold your grandfather's penknife?"

Poor James had been very unhappy about this knife, and, on hearing the stranger's question, naturally concluded his grandfather had sent him; he therefore only replied by a violent burst of tears.

"Should you like to get the knife again?"

The boy's face cleared up instantly, and he rushed out of the room; but speedily returned with a wooden box, having a small slit in the top, ingeniously contrived for the admission though not for the egress of money. He rattled its contents.

"All my own, sir; all I have saved for Christmas. I will give it all to the man, if he will let me have my poor grandfather's knife back."

"What man?" asked the barrister.

"Oh, the gipsy: he gave me a string of birds' eggs for it."

"Should you know the man now?"

"Oh, yes," said the boy; "he was so tall and black-looking."

"Well, if you will come with me, I think we may get your knife again."

The child looked wistfully at his father.

"May I go?" Of course permission was given. The farmer said he would accompany them; and a few minutes saw them driving at full speed back to the town. Leaving his young witness outside, Mr. Harvey re-entered the court.

"How does the trial go on?" asked he of a friend.

"All in favour of the prisoners: there is no doubt of their innocence and of their acquittal."

At this moment, the counsel for the prosecution stated that he had new facts to communicate, and important evidence to examine; and Mr. Harvey entered the witness-box.

We have already narrated what he had to tell.

The child was next called, evidently all surprise at the crowd and the scene; and, when first questioned, apparently too much abashed to reply. But he was naturally a fearless little fellow, and soon gave the most simple and straight-forward answers. On being asked if he understood the difference between truth and falsehood, he said—

"Yes, he knew it was very wicked to tell stories, but that he never did it."

The knife was then shewn him, which he recognised with a cry of delight; and stated, in the most artless and positive manner, how he came to sell it. He had been peeling a hazel twig, which he had taken from the copse adjoining the gipsy's tent—had cut his finger, which made him angry with the knife—at that moment the gipsy had come out of his tent, and offered him a string of birds' eggs for it—and he had accordingly made the exchange on the spot. The next question was, "Would he know the man with whom he made the exchange?"

To this he gave the same answer as he had before given to Mr. Harvey.

Unknown to the boy, who continued to look wistfully on the knife, though he made not the slightest attempt to take it, the gipsy had been so placed in court among others, as to be distinct, but not conspicuous. Little James was told to see if he could discover in the crowd the man with whom he bartered his knife.

At first he looked in the wrong direction; but the moment he turned, his eye fell upon the gipsy.

"There he is!" said he, pointing the prisoner out; and his whole frame trembling with eagerness, he clasped Mr. Harvey's hand, and exclaimed, "Oh, sir, you said I should perhaps get back my grandfather's knife: he may have all my money."

So saying, he produced his little box, which he had brought with him.

Not one in the court but marked the change of the gipsy's face when he caught sight of the child standing with the knife in his hand. He turned pale as death, and a shudder passed from head to foot. Whatever might be his feeling, it was checked and concealed almost instantly; and the look of terror was succeeded by one of such ferocity, fixed on the child, that he clung to Mr. Harvey, crying, "I do not want to have my knife again without paying."

On the female, the appearance of the child produced no effect. The testimony of James's father proved that the exchange had taken place the very day before the murder.

The chain of evidence was now complete, and the counsel for the prosecution stated that he had no more questions to put.

The prisoner was then asked whether he had aught to say in his defence, and especially in explanation of the remarkable fact so providentially brought to light? He sullenly owned to having bought the knife, but said he had dropped it out of his pocket the same day.

All were persuaded of the guilt of the man; but a strong feeling of the innocence of the woman prevailed: when suddenly the gipsy turned to his companion, and in a low voice said something in the unknown language he had before used. The effect of the words on the woman was fearful; her loud, long, heart-broken shriek rang through the court, and she sank on her knees, half, it seemed, in an attitude of supplication, half from inability to support herself. She stretched forth her arms towards the prisoner, whose face, for the first time, wore an expression of tenderness, as he gazed upon her and spoke in a singularly sweet and softly modulated tone. She rose from her knees; and whatever the last sentence was, it restored her to tranquillity. All this passed in a moment, for the prisoners were immediately surrounded, and all further communication cut off between them.

A breathless silence prevailed as the judge gave his charge to the jury. He spoke but briefly of the enormity of the crime—this murder of the aged, the defenceless, and the poor: the general horror which pervaded every one present shewed that amplification was unnecessary. The very brevity had its effect; it was as if the deed were too terrible to be dwelt upon in human hearing. He enlarged more on the folly of guilt, which is so frequently, and was in the present instance so unexpectedly awakened from its blind security, not by the chance of discovery against which it had successfully and yet vainly guarded, but by some little circumstance whose effects had never been feared. He then summed up the various facts which brought the murder home to the gipsy—the vicinity of his encampment—his hurried departure—the purchase of the knife—the clearness with which the child gave his account, and identified the prisoner—the singular carelessness which left the knife behind, as if fated that a discovery should be made—all was conclusive of the real criminal.

The guilt of the female was perhaps less indubitably proved; but when her entire subjection to her husband was taken into consideration—the impossibility of his having committed the murder without her knowledge—the secret speech which, even in the very hearing of the court, had been carried on between them—all these brought conviction of her knowledge of, if not participation in the bloody deed. If any doubt rested on the jury's mind in favour of the prisoners, it was their duty to give the suspected the full benefit of that doubt.

The jury retired; their deliberation was brief, but fatal; and a verdict of guilty was returned against both. The judge recorded the sentence, and pronounced the penalty—death.

"Death!" shrieked the female prisoner, and would have fallen with her face to the earth, but for the arm of the officer at her side. The gipsy himself burst into a torrent of blasphemies and revilings, amid which he was forced from the court.

A low moaning wind, a small sad rain, and a heavy louring sky, were meet accompaniments to the morning of execution. Slowly through the streets wound the gloomy procession; the windows, the pavement, the road, alike crowded with spectators: all the ordinary tasks of day were suspended—life pausing to gaze on death.

Her head bowed on her shoulder, as if it lacked strength to bear up its length of black hair; every shade of colour faded from both lip and cheek, till the face had the fixed and cold rigidity of a corpse, though still beautiful in feature; and the large dark eyes dilated with that look of bewildered terror you see in childhood,—the female seemed stupified and powerless from excess of dread. The gipsy sat erect in the miserable cart, and every now and then his dark ferocious eye would single out some individual for a piercing and malignant gaze: that night many a pillow was haunted by his peculiar and evil look. He evidently enjoyed the terror of his victims; and but for his fetters, none would have guessed him to be the criminal whom but one short hour separated from eternity.

The gibbet had been erected within fifty yards of Mrs. Bird's shop, and a long and dreary way there was before the murderer could reach the place of his crime and of its punishment. The usually lonely moor was covered with people; and to the left the gallows, dimly seen through the thick fog, stood out every moment more distinctly, as the mist melted into rain. The prisoners were placed upon the scaffold, and their fetters knocked off: so great was the stillness, that almost every ear heard the clank of the chains as they fell to the ground.

Again the clergyman pressed forward to offer the holy, the only hope that can visit such an hour. The gipsy pushed him aside, and actually turned towards the hangman, who, silent and unmoved, waited to perform his dreadful duty.

Suddenly roused from the state of stupefaction to which fear had reduced her, the female filled the air with shrieks. Disengaging herself from the officers, and rushing towards her husband, she clung with all her strength to his arm, imploring him, with frantic violence, not to let them kill her. He led, or rather dragged her to the front of the scaffold.

At this moment, the wind, which had been rising for some time, broke away the thick clouds behind into a line of cold clear light, which threw out the forms of the prisoners into gigantic proportions; while, blowing in the face of the people, it carried every sound forwards with singular distinctness.

Supporting the shuddering, but now speechless creature, the gipsy held her forth to the crowd.

"May the curse," said he, in a wild, shrill voice—so shrill, it was more like a scream—"May the curse of the innocent blood ye will this day shed, rest among you for ever!"

Whispering something, in a tone so low as to be only audible to her, he gave his wife, without one caress or look, to the officer. She stretched her arms towards her husband, but sank back fainting.

The hangman approached.

"Her first," exclaimed the gipsy,—the only touch of human feeling he had shewn.

While the rope was putting round her long slender neck she was quite passive; but her dying struggles were terrible. A suppressed cry of sympathy, a strange low moan—only loud from being so general—rose from the spectators: it sank into silence as the executioner turned to the gipsy. He raised his hand with a fierce gesture of menace to the crowd below, then, allowing the rope to be adjusted with utter carelessness, was launched into the air, and died seemingly without a struggle.

The black cloud, which had been sailing on, now burst, the rain came down in torrents, the crowd rapidly dispersed; and in half an hour, the moor, which had been like a vast plain of human faces, was silent and solitary—there remained only the dark gibbet high in mid-air, and the two bodies swung violently to and fro by the fierce wind.

Towards evening the fitful gleam of the lantern, and the red glare of the torch, fell upon a small, sullen-looking group of the law's officials: the hangman was among them, and his harsh, malignant face given fully to view. Hastily they dug a hole, and at the foot of the gallows buried the wretched woman; but the body of the man was made fast in chains, and left for the scorching sun, the withering wind, and the birds of prey, to preserve or to destroy. The torches were extinguished; a flickering light from the lantern shone for a while over the scene—gradually diminishing, till it finally disappeared. Long was it before human step ventured across the dismal and deserted moor.

About a week after the execution, two circumstances occurred which tended greatly to criminate the man and exculpate his wife. All the missing articles of Mrs. Bird's property were found in a hollow tree, deep in the hazel thicket, tied up in an old yellow handkerchief, which the villagers remembered seeing the gipsy wear. One fact went far to prove Rachel's innocence. Some months after, a girl, who was in service, and had come home for a few days to be present at her sister's wedding, mentioned that she had the very morning of the murder set off early for the town of A . . . . ., where she was to meet the waggon—that she had had her fortune told by the woman, and had hurried away on seeing the husband approaching from the hazel thicket, she having always feared and disliked him. This was between seven and eight o'clock, just the time when the murder must have been committed; for John Dodd, the carrier, was there about half-past eight, and the body was then warm with recent life.

The belief in the innocence of the woman gave even a deeper horror to the moor: the shop went to ruins, the path was deserted, and even now, when the gallows-tree and the body have alike gone to decay, the tradition haunts the place fresh and fearful as ever. One trace remains of the little cottage-garden. In the midst of the bare or furze-covered moor are two or three stunted gooseberry bushes: it is years since they have borne fruit, or more than a few leaves on the grey and knotted boughs; but they are still pointed out as having grown in Mrs. Bird's garden.

THERESA

"There are individuals doomed to misfortune, and such is my destiny. There must be, among the general ill-luck, some one who is the unluckiest of them all: I am that one. To be banished from Vienna before the new ballet, and simply for being absent from my quarters without leave—what I have done fifty times before with impunity! And now for Colonel Rasaki—as though he had hoarded all the malice of his life for a moment—to hold forth on the necessity of strict discipline; and to awaken me from the prettiest allegory of the West-wind suddenly being personified by Madlle. Angeline, with an order from the Emperor to try the air of this old castle—as if I were a ghost or a rat, and could possibly be the better for dust, rust, damp, and darkness!"

Count Adalbert walked up and down the gloomy chamber which had been hurriedly prepared for his reception. The high and narrow windows had been built as if quite unconscious of their proper destination, and excluded the light and air as much as possible; still, many of the panes having been broken, little streams of the rain now beating against them came driving in; and a variety of small zephyrs, in the shape of draughts, did anything but add to the Count's comfort. Half a tree would not have sufficed to fill the ample hearth, on which could just be perceived a flickering flame, almost lost in the immense volumes of smoke that rolled into the room, like waves on a beach; till Adalbert rushed in despair into the outward hall, which was inhabited by the one or two antique servitors who still remained in the large but ruinous building.

The sight of the old woman, whose wrinkled visage had driven him away in the first instance, might be shut out; now the smoke could not. Down he sat on a wooden stool, which must have been the first attempt ever made at a seat, so irregular were its shape and movements. This he drew to a table, whereon a most disconsolate supper was spread: twice the visitor looked down, to see whether he was cutting the meat or the wooden trencher.

Like most other young men, Count Adalbert had relations who conceived they knew better what was good for him than he did himself; and his uncle—whose experience was certainly very efficacious as a warning, and who believed that an error was easier to be prevented than remedied—on perceiving the young Count's predilection for the prettiest dancer that had ever illuminated the horizon of Vienna, deemed that some rouleaux, and even a diamond necklace, would be saved by his nephew's being introduced to the historical records of his family, in which the old Castle of Aremberg occupied a distinguished place. Advantage was accordingly taken of a slight breach of military observance, and the delinquent forced to leave Vienna at a quarter of an hour's notice—quite unsuspicious how active his uncle had been for his good. Had Adalbert been aware of this most fatherly act, it is probable his guardian would have more than shared the execrations which the exile lavished in his inmost heart on fate, Colonel Rasaki, nay even on the august person of the Emperor.

A long ride had completely fatigued him, and he resolved to postpone his discontents.

"I shall have time enough to grumble," thought he, as he followed the lighted pine-splinter—the only taper the place afforded—to the state chamber. The moths flew out of the tapestry as he entered—they had half devoured the court of Solomon, no more "in all his glory;" the green velvet hangings of the enormous bed had shared the same fate; and Adalbert was again driven to the hall, where he fell asleep thinking of suicide, and awoke dreaming of Angeline, whose image, however, instantly took flight before the melancholy reality of the old castle.

Yet, a week had not elapsed before Adalbert thought the said castle very well for a change, and the neighbourhood delightful. The truth is, he had fallen in love—as pleasant a method of passing time in the country as any young gentleman could devise.

Wandering in search of the beauties of Nature—(people who have nothing else to do, become picturesque in self-defence)—he met with one of her beauties indeed, the loveliest peasant girl that ever "made sunshine in a shady place." A scarlet cloth cap, trimmed with fur, partly covered a profusion of fair hair, which was parted on the soft forehead, and fell in bright and natural ringlets on the neck; her dress was of grey serge, and short enough to shew a foot and ankle such as not even the rude country shoes could disguise; her cheek had the bright beaming crimson of early youth and morning exercise; and her deep blue eyes shone with the vivacity of uncurbed gaiety and unbroken spirits. She came along, bearing a willow basket of wood-strawberries and wild blossoms, with a dancing step, and a lively song on her lips, singing in the very gladness of her heart.

The strawberries led to an acquaintance—Adalbert was thirsty, and Theresa (for such was her name) generous: she divided her fruit with the stranger, eagerly pressing the best upon him, in all the frank and earnest good-nature of a child. She was too simple, and too much accustomed to meet with kindness from every one, to be bashful.

They arrived at the cottage, where Theresa's mother made Adalbert as welcome as herself; and in a few days, whether seated by her side as she turned her spinning-wheel of an evening, or with her when wandering in search of wild flowers and fruit, the contented exile and the beautiful peasant were constantly together. The dame was exceedingly quick in observing their love, which she seemed to consider quite natural. Though very ignorant, she had seen something of society beyond their own valley and its peasantry, and at once discovered that the Count was their superior: but the goodness and loveliness of her child entitled her, in the old woman's eyes, to be a princess at least.

Theresa was the most guileless creature, and had never dreamt of love till she felt it; the world to her was bounded by the wild moor and deep wood which surrounded their cottage. The only human beings she had ever beheld were the ancient domestics at the Castle, and a few of the peasants far poorer than themselves; for they had many comforts, which their neighbours eyed with much suspicion and some envy. Learning she had none, for neither mother nor daughter could read; but knowledge she had acquired. She knew all the legends and ballads of the country by heart; these gave their poetry to her naturally vivid imagination; and the imagination refines both feeling and manner. Having lived in absolute seclusion, she had nothing of that coarseness caught from familiar intercourse unrestrained by the delicacies of polished life. Her companions had been the bird and the blossom, her songs, and her thoughts; and if the poet's dream of unsophisticated, yet refined nature, was ever realised, it was in that sweet and innocent maiden. Her love for Adalbert was a singular blending of childishness and romance: now her inward delight would find vent in buoyant laughter, and the playfulness of a young fawn bounding along the sunny glades of a forest: but oftener would she sink into a deep and tender silence—as if conscious that a new and even fearful existence had opened upon her—and gaze in his face, till her eyes were averted to conceal the large tears that had insensibly gathered in them. They had been acquainted with each other one whole fortnight, when the old priest at Hartzburg was called upon to marry the handsomest couple that had ever stood before the image of the Madonna!

If we did but know how we rush into one evil while seeking to avoid another, we should have no resolution to shun any thing. Could Count von Hermanstadt have anticipated that the fascinating dancer was far less dangerous than the then unknown peasant, his nephew would never have been ordered to the Castle of Aremberg. Little either could he dream, that the incognito he had himself enjoined, would have been found so useful and agreeable by his nephew. For Count von Hermanstadt, though very willing that Adalbert should take the Emperor's displeasure for granted, was not desirous that others of a court where the sovereign's favour was every thing, should likewise take it for granted.

The first three weeks of Adalbert's married life passed very delightfully away, his position was one of such complete novelty: the cottage really was pleasanter than the castle; and if Theresa's beauty might have been a model for the painter, as the sweet colours flitted over her face, in like manner the many emotions that now disturbed the calm of a mind hitherto so tranquil and so glad, might have been a study for the philosopher. But Adalbert's previous habits had been ill-fitted to make their present state one of security—nay, his very youth was an obstacle; for in youth it seems so natural to love and be beloved, that we know not how to value as we ought the first devotion of the entire and trusting heart. Moreover, he had lived in a world of sarcasm; and Theresa's ignorance, which, now they were by themselves, was but a source of amusement, would, as he was aware, have been fertile matter of ridicule in society—ridicule, too, which must have reflected on him. Besides, all the prejudices of ancestry had, from infancy, been grafted on his mind—and he would as soon have thought of throwing his companion into the river on whose waters they were gazing, each on the mirrored face of the other, as of presenting her at Vienna. And yet that would have been the more merciful course. What was life whose affections were wounded, and whose hopes were destroyed? And such was the life to which Adalbert was about to leave her. It came at last.

Mademoiselle Angeline's engagement had now drawn to its close: the manager offered to have the stage paved with ducats, if she would but give him one night more—the tenth muse was inexorable; and the day she departed for Paris, Adalbert received his recall to Vienna. To say he felt no regret, would be doing him scant justice—to say he felt much, would be more than the truth. Once or twice he thought of taking Theresa with him; but from this step he shrank for many reasons, not the least of which was, that a lingering impulse of good forbade his transplanting the pure and beautiful flower to wither and die in the thick and blighting atmosphere of the city: besides, he should often be able to visit Aremberg. He told them of important business—of a speedy return—and said all that has been so often and so vainly said in the hour of parting. He threw his horse's bridle over his arm, and Theresa walked with him along the little forest path which led to the road.

Adalbert was almost angry that she shewed none of the passionate despair, whose complaints he had nerved himself to meet: pale, silent, she clasped his hand a little more tenderly, she gazed on his face even more intently, than usual; and yet these tokens of sorrow she seemed trying to suppress. It never entered her imagination that any entreaty of hers could alter their position—that any prayer could have prolonged Adalbert's stay for an hour; but every effort was directed to conceal her own grief: she felt so acutely the least sign of his suffering, that she only wished to spare him the sight of hers. At last he mounted his horse—once he looked back—Theresa was leaning against the old oak-tree for support, watching his progress—she caught his look, and as she interpreted it into an intention of returning, she held out her hands, and he could see the light come again to her eye and the colour to her cheek, while she sprang forward breathless with expectation; he, however, averted his head, and spurred his steed to its utmost swiftness: he did not see her sink on the earth—the strength which had sustained her had gone with her husband.

Youth's first acquaintance with sorrow is a terrible thing—before time has taught, what it will surely teach, that grief is our natural portion, at once transitory and eternal. But the first lesson is the severest—we have not then looked among our fellows, and seen that suffering is general; and we feel as if marked out by fate for misery that has no parallel. Theresa felt more acutely every hour, how wide a gulf had opened between her present and past existence: her girlhood had passed for ever; she took no pleasure in any of her former pursuits; she had put away childish things; and nothing had arisen to supply their place, save one memory haunted but by one image. Days, weeks elapsed, and Adalbert returned not—her sleep was broken by a thousand fanciful terrors; but one fear had taken possession of her mother Ursaline's mind—that the stranger was false; and bitterly did she lament that she had ever intrusted him with the happiness of her precious child.

"And yet I did it for the best!" she would piteously exclaim, whenever her eye fell on the pale cheek of her daughter.

"He is come, my mother!" exclaimed Theresa, bounding one evening into the cottage with a long-unaccustomed lightness of heart and step. Though eager to spring down the path and meet him, yet, amid all the forgetfulness of joy, she had bethought her of her aged parent, and returned that she too might share the happiness of their meeting. They hurried out, and three horsemen were riding up the valley—one much in advance of the others.

"Mother, it is a stranger!" with difficulty articulated Theresa, and, sick at heart, clung to her arm for support.

The rider was full in sight, when, with a shriek that roused her daughter, Ursaline exclaimed, "Now the blessed saints be good unto us, but it is my old master—I should know him amid a thousand!"

The words were scarcely uttered, when the horseman dismounted at a rough part of the road, and, flinging his bridle to his attendants, approached alone. He was a tall, stately, and austere-looking man, seemingly about fifty, and one who apparently knew the place well. Ursaline dropped on her knee; he raised her kindly, and, following the direction of her look, turned and clasped Theresa in his arms.

"My child! my sweet child!" and he gazed long and earnestly on her beautiful face.

"Your father, the Baron von Haitzinger," murmured Ursaline.

But as our explanation will be more brief than one broken in upon by words of wonder, regret, and affection, we will proceed to it; holding that explanation, like advice, should be of all convenient shortness. So much good luck had the Baron von Haitzinger had during the first thirty years of his life, that fortune seemed under the necessity of crowding an inordinate portion of evil into a small space, in order to make up for lost time. The same day brought him intelligence of his wife's desertion, and of his attaintment as a traitor; and, further, that this accusation had been chiefly brought about by the intrigues of his former partner. A price being set on a man's head, usually makes him very speedy in his movements; and the Baron fled from his castle with the rapidity of life and death, but not unaccompanied. Wrapt in his mantle he bore with him their only child, a little girl of two years old. As boys, he and the Count von Hermanstadt had often hunted in the forests around Aremberg; his own foster-sister had married one of the dependants of the family; and to the care of Ursaline, now a widow, he resolved to intrust his Theresa. Never should she owe her nurture to her mother—no, she should grow up pure and unsophisticated as the wild flowers on the heath beside her dwelling. Ursaline gave the required oath of secrecy, and took the charge.

Years and years of exile had passed over the Baron's head; his wife died—that was some comfort; and at length, a new emperor, together with the indefatigable efforts of his friend, Von Hermanstadt, procured the establishment of his innocence, the repeal of his banishment, and the restoration of his estate. His first act was to throw himself at the feet of his gracious sovereign, his second to depart in search of his child.

We have stated, it was the Baron's wish that Theresa should be brought up in ignorance and simplicity; but, as usually happens when our wishes are fulfilled, he was disappointed and somewhat dismayed on finding that she could not even read; and that instead of French, now the only language tolerated at Vienna, and which alone he had spoken for years—his exile having been alleviated by a constant residence at Paris—his child was unable to greet him save in the gutturals of her native German. Aghast at the ridicule the result of his experiment might entail upon him, he hurried to his family estate: here, having engaged a French governess and a professor of singing, he resolved to keep Theresa in perfect seclusion for two years longer. Somewhat reluctantly, Ursaline accompanied them; for her dread of their secret being discovered almost overcame her distress at the bare thought of her foster-child.

"The Baron will kill us if he hears of your marriage—and yet I did it for the best: I thought he must be dead, and I knew you ought to marry none but a noble. Who could have thought Count Adalbert would have proved so false-hearted?"

Such were the constant lamentations of the old nurse whenever they were alone: but the secret she had to keep was too much for her; and six weeks after leaving their cottage, Ursaline was safe from Von Haitzinger's anger in the grave.

Theresa wept for her long and bitterly: many sorrows took the semblance of one. Treated as a child, offered the amusements and the rewards of a child, when her heart was full of the grief and care of a woman—hourly she was more and more thrown upon herself. Her father, who considered every moment lost which was not given to the pursuit of education, debarred himself from her society. It was a sacrifice, but to Theresa it appeared choice; and he thus repelled the confidence which kindness and familiar intercourse might have encouraged. She soon took an interest in the employments selected for her—they served to divert her attention from a remembrance that grew continually more painful. Every step she gained in knowledge, every experience brought by reading or conversation, but served to shew her more fully the difficulty of her position.

Love is the destiny of a woman's life, and hers had been sealed on the threshold of existence: it was too late now to change the colour of or alter the past. Theresa's greatest enjoyment was to wander through the lonely gardens: though the leaf and the flower could never more be to her the companions they had been, still, when alone, they aided her in recalling the days when they were mute witnesses to vows which had the common fate of being kept but by one. The difference between herself and those of her own age consisted in this, that they looked to the future, she dwelt upon the past; they hoped, she only remembered.

The young Countess's instructors were loud in their praises of her docility and progress; the French governess remarking, "Mademoiselle est pleine des talens et des graces; mais elle est si triste et si silencieuse."

The two years passed, and Theresa was to accompany her father to Vienna. The Baron von Haitzinger, who had never quite recovered the shock of finding that his daughter could only speak German, and could neither read nor write, was utterly unprepared for the sensation she produced on her introduction into society. Theresa at twenty more than realised the promise of seventeen; yet it is singular how much the character of her beauty was changed. She had been a glad, bright, buoyant creature, with a cheek like a rose, a mouth radiant with smiles, and the golden curls dancing in sunny profusion over the blushes they shaded. Now her hair and eyes were much darker, her cheek was pale, and the general cast of her face melancholy and thoughtful; her step was still light, but slow—it was urged on no longer by inward buoyancy: and if a painter, three years before, would have chosen her as a model for the youngest of the Graces, he would now have selected her for the loveliest of the Muses— so ethereal, so intellectual was that sad and expressive countenance. Her father was charmed with the ease and self-possession of her manner—the perfection of beautiful repose: true, it was broken in upon by none of the flatterings of girlish vanity, none of the slight yet keen excitements of a season given to gaiety.

The Countess was wholly indifferent to the scene that surrounded her—to its pleasure and its triumph; she had a standard of her own by which she measured enjoyment, and found what was here deemed pleasure by others, to be vapid and worthless; and now, more than ever, the image of Adalbert rose present to her mind. She compared him with the many cavaliers about her; and the comparison was, as it ever is, in favour of the heart's earliest idol. Even when unconsciously yielding to the influence exercised by light, music, and a glittering crowd, Theresa would start back, and muse on what might be the fate of Adalbert at that very moment; for, with a confidence belonging to youth and woman, she admitted any suggestion rather than the obvious one of his inconstancy. Two or three brilliant conquests cost her a sleepless night and a pale cheek; but as her father always acquiesced in a prompt refusal, she gradually became happy in the belief that he did not desire her marriage.

One evening all Vienna was assembled at a reunion given by the French Ambassador. Dazzling with jewels, and looking her very loveliest, Theresa was seated beside the lady who accompanied her, when her eye suddenly rested on Adalbert. A dense crowd was between them, but the platform on which he was standing enabled him to see over their heads; and he was evidently gazing on her. With a faint cry, she half started from her seat—fortunately she was unobserved; and again sinking back in her chair, she endeavoured to collect her scattered spirits from their first confusion of surprise and delight. Her astonishment had yet to be increased. The Baron appeared on the scene, greeted the stranger most cordially, and arm in arm they descended among the throng. At intervals she caught sight of his splendid uniform; it came nearer and nearer: at last they emerged from a very ocean of velvet and plumes, and her father addressed her—

"Theresa, my love! I am most anxious to present to you the nephew of my oldest friend, Prince Ernest von Hermanstadt." Adalbert, or Ernest, bowed most admiringly it is true, but without the slightest token of recognition. Faint, breathless, Theresa sought in vain to speak.

"You look pale, my child," said her father; "the heat is too much for you. Do, Ernest, try to make your way with her to the window, and I will get a glass of water."

Theresa felt her hand drawn lightly through the arm to which she had so often clung, and the Prince with some difficulty conveyed her to the window. There they stood alone for some minutes, before the Baron could rejoin them; yet not by word or sign did her companion imply a previous knowledge. His manner was most gentle, most attentive; but it was that of a perfect stranger.

Theresa drank the glass of water, and, by a strong effort, recalled her presence of mind. She looked in Prince Ernest's face—it was no mistake; every feature of that noble and striking countenance was too deeply treasured for forgetfulness. Her father, by continually addressing her, shewed how anxious he was for her to join in the conversation. At last she trusted her voice with a few brief words; the Prince listened to them eagerly, but, it was evident, only with present admiration.

They remained together the rest of the evening, and the Prince von Hermanstadt handed her to the Baron's carriage.

"What do you think of my young favourite?" asked her father, as they entered their abode. "But I hate unnecessary mysteries, so shall tell you at once, that in Prince Ernest you see your destined husband: you have been betrothed from your birth. This, however, is no time to talk over family matters, for you look fatigued to death."

Theresa retired to her chamber, her head dizzy with surprise and sorrow. She had gleaned enough from the conversation to discover that Ernest's absence from his country had been entirely voluntary—that she had known him under a feigned name—therefore, from the very first he had been deceiving her. Strange that till this moment her heart had never admitted the belief of his falsehood! As she paced her room, she caught sight of her whole-length figure in the glass: then rose upon her memory her own reflection as she had seen it shadowed in the river near her early home, and the change in herself struck her forcibly.

"I marvel that he knew me not?—it were far greater marvel had he known me."

She looked long and earnestly in the mirror; a rich colour rose to her cheek, and the light flashed from her eyes—

"What if I could make him love me now? and then let him feel only the faintest part of what I have felt!" But the last words were so softly uttered, that they sounded like anything rather than a denunciation of revenge.

The next day and the next saw Ernest a constant visitor; and Theresa in vain sought to hide from herself the truth, that she felt a keen pleasure in observing how much more suitable her new self was to her former lover. Then they had nothing, now they had so much in common with each other; they read together, they talked together; and Hermanstadt was delighted with the melancholy and thoughtful style of her conversation.

The summer was now advancing, and Haitzinger proposed visiting the Castle. Thither the whole party adjourned; the two elder Barons—for Ernest's uncle had now joined them—leaving the young people almost entirely to themselves. Here Theresa could not but perceive that Ernest grew daily depressed; sometimes he would leave her abruptly, and she would afterwards learn that for hours he had been wandering alone.

One evening, while walking in the old picture-gallery, Theresa turned to the window to admire the luxuriant growth of a parasitic plant, whose drooping white flowers hung in numberless fragrant clusters. Ernest approached to her side, and they leant from the casement—both mute with the same emotion, though from different causes. Suddenly he broke silence, and Theresa again listened to the avowal of his love. But now the voice was low and broken, and he spoke mournfully and hopelessly; for in the same hour in which he owned his passion for the Countess, he also acknowledged to her his marriage with the peasant. Ernest had, in truth, been spoilt by circumstances; his conquests had been too easy, and he had mistaken vanity and interest for love. But a deep and true feeling elevates and purifies the heart into which it enters. His passion for Theresa brought back his better nature; and he now bitterly deplored the misery he must have caused the young and forsaken creature, whose happiness he had destroyed by such thoughtless cruelty. "The sacrifice I now make may well be held an atonement."

He turned to leave the gallery as he spoke, but Theresa's voice arrested his steps.

"I have long known your history. Prince Ernest—long looked for this confession. Your wife is now in the Castle; I will prepare her for an interview—from her you must seek your pardon."

She was gone before Von Hermanstadt recovered his breath. It would be vain to say what were his thoughts during the succeeding minutes; shame, surprise—something, too, of pity blended with regret. He had not moved from the spot, when the Countess's page put a note into his hand.

"I do not wish to let my father know all yet: join us at the end of the acacia wood—your wife there awaits your arrival.—Theresa."

The Prince obeyed the summons mechanically—as in dreams we obey some strange power. A sharp angle in the walk brought him, before he was aware, to the place; and there, as though he had but just parted from her, stood his wife, leaning for support against the old oak. She wore the scarlet cap broidered with fur, the grey stuff dress, and the plaited apron: her beautiful profile was half turned towards him.

"Theresa!" he whispered; when, starting at the face, which was now completely given to view, he exclaimed, "Is it possible?" for he saw instantly that it was the Countess before him.

"Yes, Adalbert—or Ernest—by which name shall I claim you?" And the next moment she was in his arms.

Confession and forgiveness followed of course; though the Baron von Haitzinger resolved that he would give no encouragement to his grand-daughters' being brought up in unsophisticated seclusion, as it rarely happens that two experiments of the same kind turn out well. Still, it is but justice to state, that Theresa never had any further occasion to regret that her husband's heart was once lost and twice won.